D1269834

THE ATLANTIC TUNNEL

Deep beneath the floor of the Atlantic Ocean, scientists and engineers attempt the most daring and audacious scientific project of all time: the construction of an undersea tunnel between Great Britain and Canada; linking Land's End with Labrador. Canadian and British teams work simultaneously at either end, to converge in the middle. Using scientific methods to fight the crushing pressure and geological and marine perils involved, the brave workers face a far greater hazard — the danger within — from saboteurs!

JOHN RUSSELL FEARN

THE ATLANTIC TUNNEL

Complete and Unabridged

LINFORD
Leicester

First published in Great Britain

First Linford Edition
published 2009

British Library CIP Data

Fearn, John Russell, *1908 – 1960.*
　　The Atlantic tunnel - - (Linford mystery library)
　　1. Underwater tunnels- -Atlantic Ocean- -
　　Design and construction- -Fiction. 2. Sabotage
　　- -Fiction. 3. Detective and mystery stories.
　　4. Large type books.
　　I. Title II. Series III. Fearn, John Russell,
　　1908 – 1960. Land's End – Labrador.
　　823.9'12–dc22

　　ISBN 978–1–84782–751–7

Published by
F. A. Thorpe (Publishing)
Anstey, Leicestershire

Set by Words & Graphics Ltd.
Anstey, Leicestershire
Printed and bound in Great Britain by
T. J. International Ltd., Padstow, Cornwall

This book is printed on acid-free paper

1

The accident

Martin Astley sat looking intently at the metal. He was not even aware of the immense physical laboratory around him, or of the men and women technicians hurrying to and fro on their various errands. For Martin Astley time had stopped — for the moment.

Presently he picked up the square of metal in his hands and turned it over and over in the searching rays of the desk lamp. The metal reflected back smoothly as the light caught it — a curious iridescence of colours somewhat reminiscent of shot silk.

'Amazing!' Astley breathed to himself. 'Absolutely amazing! That a thing like this could happen by accident!'

For indeed it had. Due to a mixup in the foundries, this foot-square of gleaming metal had come into being. It ought to have been a refined and highly tempered steel, but instead it was something else — something with the smoothness of satin, the lightness of aluminium, and the hardness of . . . Well, the hardness of nothing else on earth. It had withstood the maximum pressure of the Lovelace Engineering Works' mightiest testing machines. It had come out with hardly a discolouration from deliberately planned nuclear impacts. It was the wonder metal — Steel-X — and the toughest thing that had ever been produced.

Astley put the metal down again, and sat back to think. As the chief metallurgic scientist to the huge engineering concern he could take all the time he wanted and nobody would dare bother him — mainly because he was in the unique position that nobody could get along without his genius. But here was something that even he had never bargained for. In working out the formula for a highly tempered steel he had unwittingly produced — or rather the foundries had — this incredible stuff with the phenomenal hardness.

And Astley knew exactly what he was going to do now. He had never been slow to grasp an opportunity, and one like this just yelled out loud for negotiation. So Astley ceased his meditations, picked up the metal square, and headed through the wilderness of laboratory to the executive offices. He knocked on the glass panels of one imposing door in particular, identified with the inscription 'Douglas Lovelace, Governing Director.'

Quietly, Astley entered the plushy office as a gruff baritone bade him come in. He went across to the desk and Douglas Lovelace, financial boss and emperor of the engineering concern, looked at him expectantly — a short, bald man in the sixties with a mouth as sentimental as a steel trap.

'Well, Martin, what's on your mind?'

Astley placed the satiny metal square on the desk.

'This,' he said, seating himself with the easy familiarity of a trusted employee. 'I think there's a fortune in it, but big business isn't my line. I'm just a scientist. But it's certainly your line so I'm dropping a ripe plum right in your lap.'

Lovelace picked up the square and examined it. Then he aimed a questioning glance.

'What is it? Steel with a new polish?'

'I'd say it's an entirely new steel. Steel-X if you like. I haven't had the chance to examine the ingredients involved because it came into being by accident. It's a fortuity, D.L., the composite result of a new tempered steel mixed up with God knows what.'

Lovelace sat back. 'You're the scientist. Where does this get us?'

'I don't know, but even I can see that a new metal of such beauty and hardness should have a ready market.'

'Beauty I grant you: the sheen is remarkable. But where does the hardness come in? What's its rating?'

'It doesn't even show a fracture when placed edgewise and subjected to a strain of a hundred thousand tons.'

Lovelace's mouth opened, but he did not speak. He sat staring at the lean-faced, fortyish man with untidy hair who had made the pronouncement.

'Further,' Astley added, 'it doesn't even show discolouration when placed in a nuclear chamber and bombarded with all the violence of an H-bomb explosion. Nothing — absolutely nothing — can make any impression on it!'

'And it was an accident?' Lovelace exclaimed.

Astley smiled. 'The really great discoveries usually are.'

'Who else knows about this? They must know something at the foundries, surely?'

'I don't think they do.' Astley meditated over it. 'No; I'm pretty sure they don't. They used the ores for my original formula of a new highly tempered steel, then due to some mistake in the moulds another lot of ore got thrown in. I'm investigating it, tracing every scrap of metal back to its source. When I have everything I'll know what happened — and then only. There isn't another man in this organization clever enough to put Humpty Dumpty together again outside me.'

Lovelace began to grin. 'Good man! Which leaves it as your own pigeon

— which you are handing on to me?'

'We trust each other, D.L., and always have done. I know you'll do the right thing financially by me when you work something out. I have the formula: you have the money and business sense. Between us we ought to hatch something pretty startling.'

Lovelace got up restlessly from the desk and began to rove around his office — his custom when absorbed in thought. Astley waited, an acid-stained finger tracing along his lower lip, his untidy brown hair straggling across his wide forehead.

Presently Lovelace said, 'There's one thing bothering me. If this metal is so damned tough how are we going to fashion it? Mould it? Isn't that a drawback?'

'Not at all. It only gets like this when cool and withdrawn from the furnace. In the original state it's as malleable as anything else. Something happens when it gets into the high temperatures. Obviously it will be cast into the required mould before the final heating takes place.'

'Mmmm . . . Have you anything in mind for the stuff?'

'Offhand, quite a multitude of things. For instance, it would make marvellous shelters against bomb attack in any future nuclear war. Or it would look just as fantastically beautiful forming the inner wall of a lounge. Think of that stuff in your own lounge, D.L. — it would catch the lights and gleam like a million diamonds.'

'It's an angle,' Lovelace admitted. 'But we want something big, to draw the attention of the whole world to the stuff . . . '

'Better let me find out first what the stuff really is. I don't anticipate trouble, but I'd prefer to know what I'm doing.'

'Trouble?'

'Steel-X may be an unstable element,' Astley said. 'If Steel-X is unstable, we shan't dare to use it.'

'Why?' Lovelace demanded bluntly.

'Because at any moment it might change its atomic build-up and collapse. However — ' Astley got to his feet. 'I don't anticipate anything like that. But just content yourself with ideas until I have given the metal a complete analysis. Then we'll know what we're doing.'

Lovelace nodded his bald head but did not say anything. He seemed to be dreaming of things far away . . .

For a week, whilst Douglas Lovelace mulled over all kinds of uses to which Steel-X could be put, Martin Astley conducted an investigation as to how the stuff had come to be made in the first place. For the time being he dropped his normal work as the company's chief metallurgical scientist and concentrated solely on the problem of the wonder metal. He paid innumerable visits to the firm's foundry master, made endless calculations in his laboratory, and finally performed a variety of tests on the metal that had been created. When at last he was satisfied he took the results to Lovelace — and, as usual, because it was Astley speaking, Lovelace listened carefully to all that was said.

'Firstly,' Astley said, 'you can disabuse your mind of any ideas about Steel-X being unstable. It isn't. The main thing is that it's solid, very unlikely to change its state, and has a life of thousands of years.'

Lovelace heaved a sigh of relief, and waited.

'As to how it came into being,' Astley continued. 'I've found it was the outcome of a catalyst.'

'I may be dumb,' Lovelace admitted, 'but what in hell is a catalyst?'

'A catalyst, scientifically, may be said to be a property which affects another property in an unpredictable manner, whilst itself it remains unaltered.'

'Stop the high-flown language, Mart, and give it to me straight!'

'I'm trying to,' Astley said patiently. 'To put it another way — the ores for my new tempered steel went into the furnace in the usual way, in a mould. During that process another mould got upset into ours. It did not actually mingle with our substance but it affected it in an odd way, giving it a strength, sheen, and lightness beyond anything known before. On examination, under the electron microscope, Steel-X reveals places when the catalyst has been absorbed into the general pattern, but they're distinct spots, as clear under the microscope as currants in a cake.'

'Meaning what, then? That they'll be flaws?'

'Not at all. They're only in an infinitesimal percentage compared to the whole mass of metal. No — because of their presence at the time of maximum heat they became fused into Steel-X and produced their catalytic effect. Without them, we'd have tempered steel as planned originally. With them, we have Steel-X.'

Lovelace reflected. 'And can the 'ingredients' of this what-you-call-it, this catalyst, be duplicated for future use?'

'Endlessly!' Astley smiled. 'Several elements were involved and were mainly waste products being smelted down for the cheap commercial market, but I know what they were and the quantities used in comparison with Steel-X in the raw state. I can duplicate the effect any time it's needed . . . Now you know. I've done my part. What ideas have you got?'

Lovelace spread his hands. 'The greatest idea of the age, Mart! When you were here before I said we needed something that would draw the attention of the whole world to Steel-X. I think I've got the answer ... We're going to bore our way to Labrador!'

'We're going to — *what?*' Astley stared fixedly; at which Lovelace gave a broad grin.

'I thought it would shake you — but I'm serious. We're going to construct a tunnel under the Atlantic Ocean — the greatest engineering project that any organization ever envisaged. If that doesn't bring Steel-X into prominence nothing will.'

Completely caught off his guard the scientist still stared in amazement. Lovelace went on talking with the assurance of a man who has paid infinite thought to his plans.

'I've had two weeks to think this out,' he explained. 'Two weeks in which to think of something that advertises Steel-X, uses it to the full, benefits everybody, and provides a colossal commercial return. Also something that will at last link two parts of the British Commonwealth in

11

everyday unity, more solidly than 'phone, air, sea.'

Astley found his voice. 'Look, D.L., I know you have a strong patriotic streak, but — isn't this going a bit far?'

'I don't see why,' Lovelace argued. 'I don't claim that the idea of an Atlantic Tunnel is original: it's been mooted several times by big engineering concerns, but an estimate of expense has killed the idea. But this time, with this new metal, it's a practical possibility. Steel-X for the Tunnel itself, a metal that will withstand the immense pressures, and look good at the same time. Steel-X for the drills that will gnaw their way through the rock . . . ' Lovelace stopped and drew a deep breath. 'It's the greatest dream ever, Mart, and you and I are the ones to make it a reality. In five years — ten at the outside — we can link England with Canada and thereby start the unification of the British Commonwealth of nations.'

Astley was silent again. He had expected something big to come from Steel-X but he had never anticipated this.

He knew too that in a thousand and one things Douglas Lovelace betrayed his enormous patriotism in political and commercial affairs. He believed, and always had, in the vast potentialities of the British Commonwealth.

'You're wondering — why Labrador?' Lovelace asked presently, and Astley nodded.

'Frankly, yes. Why not London-New York, and link America with Britain?'

'For two reasons. Firstly, Canada has all the potentialities of the United States, and is also of British root; and secondly, from the engineering aspect, it will be easier to drive a Tunnel under the so-called Telegraphic Plateau between the British Isles and Labrador than it will under the vast deeps of the Atlantic proper. Either way the job will be gargantuan, but I can visualise that it will succeed. I want geologists and engineers to report on the possibilities and let me study them. And I want you to sketch out drafts of drills and tunnels, made of Steel-X, and calculated to stand the ultimate of pressure and strain.'

Astley smiled rather wryly. 'And what of my other work?'

'Other work?'

'I'm chief metallurgist and scientist of this organization, and I have plenty on my plate at the moment due to the time I've lost.'

'You've lost no time at all, man: you've produced results in that you've satisfactorily analyzed Steel-X. As for your other jobs, give them to the lab boys and let them do the worrying. Nothing's as important as this Tunnel project and I want you to give it your undivided attention. Right?'

'Right!' Astley conceded, rising.

'As soon as practicable we'll have a meeting about the business — but before we do I want every detail from the experts.' Astley moved towards the door, then Lovelace's voice checked him.

'One last observation, Mart. Steel-X is yours, and I'll see to it that it is made yours legally. After that you'll name your own price for the exclusive use of it by this organization.'

'Thanks.' Astley smiled a little. 'I don't

doubt we'll have no difficulty in coming to terms.'

* * *

From that moment onwards neither Martin Astley nor Douglas Lovelace lost any time — but they both worked in a different way.

Whilst Astley lost himself in a wilderness of draft drawings and more or less sat motionless with his mind working at top speed, Lovelace was everywhere at once — paying either personal visits to different places or else relying on the medium of telecommunications. His enormous enthusiasm carried him through, because he had hold of a mighty dream and saw a real chance of bringing it to life. It was up to him to win his point by the sheer force of his personality: it was up to him to gather together those whom he thought necessary to a major conference at the Lovelace Engineering Works.

He rallied to his banner the top men in their particular professions, such as Herbert Gaulter, the world's leading

15

authority on geology and earth-lore; Boyd Exmoor, probably the best mining engineer in Britain — and Henry Saunders, his opposite number in Canada, even if there was a difference of twenty years between them. To these estimable gentlemen there were added Brown and Schuster, top-line metal and machinery tycoons with an interest in transport and railways; and Professor Albride, an experienced ambassador for the World Nuclear Power Authority. These six men — making eight when Lovelace and Astley were included — represented the nucleus of the Land's End-Labrador project, and as such, when Lovelace had completed his studies of the scheme, they met one fine May morning in the Lovelace Boardroom to discuss the preliminary details.

Present also were three other individuals, two young men and a pretty woman in the early twenties. In his introduction Lovelace explained the men away as representatives of the British and Canadian Governments respectively, whilst the girl was apparently Judith Saunders, daughter of Canadian engineer Henry Saunders, and his secretary and a mining engineer in her own right. Which fact interested Boyd Exmoor, the British mining engineer, more than somewhat. A tall, square-packed man with a dogged though still young face, he kept watching Judith Saunders attentively as she talked with a bright intelligence with one or other of the men either side of her.

'Now, my friends . . .' Lovelace, at the head of the big conference table, looked about him with serene confidence. 'Now to details. All of you know the object of this meeting — that there is on foot a project to drive an undersea bore from Land's End to Labrador, our route passing under the existing Telegraph Plateau. Previous projects have named a different route — namely Liverpool to New York. All of them failed, mainly because of lack of finance. This time I live in high hopes that that problem will not let us down.'

Lovelace's eyes strayed to Brown and Schuster, but these gentlemen of enormous wealth and influence were both looking at the table top, waiting for the next. Not a muscle twitched on their poker faces.

'To the main facts first,' Lovelace went on. 'The basic necessity of a project like this is a metal capable of standing the enormous pressures of passing under the sea bed, and drills of a hardness sufficient to gnaw through the toughest rock. That metal we have in Steel-X.'

A glance at Martin Astley and he took up the story, explaining in detail in his unhurried voice. Eyebrows rose as Astley gave the figures that Steel-X could withstand, but beyond that there was as yet no comment.

'Detailed discussion can come later,' Lovelace resumed. 'For the moment I am confining myself to the broad facts — and here they are.' He picked up a sheaf of notes from the desk. 'The Bore, as it will be called, will commence at Land's End in Cornwall, and end at a point between Zoar and Hopedale on the Labrador coast. Or, more correctly, the Canadian and British teams will begin work simultaneously at either end and meet in

18

the middle, all of which involves a distance of approximately 2,500 miles, and a descent to the maximum depth of 2,000 fathoms of ocean — or 12,000 feet. For the sake of example let us say that our maximum depth will be 12,500 feet, which will take us well under the bed of the Atlantic.'

Saunders — big and mid-fiftyish — figured roughly on his scratch pad and then stroked his square, immaculate chin.

'You've considered carefully the pressures bearing upon this theoretical Tunnel at 12,500 feet, I take it?'

'In detail,' Lovelace answered. 'Steel-X can withstand that, and would still be safe and sound at twice the depth.'

'12,500 feet is the hell of a way down,' commented Boyd Exmoor, with a dubious glance at his Canadian opposite number. 'Not quite half the height of Everest, if you want an example. I've certainly never penetrated to even a fraction of that depth.'

'Naturally,' Lovelace agreed, unmoved. 'Even so, gentlemen, you are not expected to attempt this feat unprepared, or with a bucket and spade. All the labour and machines you want will be supplied — all the money you need — and full permission is granted by Canada and Britain as these two Government representatives will confirm.'

The two ambassadors nodded gravely but said nothing.

'And what,' Exmoor asked, taking his eyes from Judith Saunders, 'can we expect in the way of trouble?'

'That's my field,' responded Herbert Gaulter, the geologist. 'There is no reason to anticipate anything of an impassable nature. My own findings are given in detail in my papers here, which you'll want to study at your leisure — but as a broad picture I would say that as you move outwards and downwards you'll encounter the usual kind of sedimentary and igneous rocks. Chalk, limestone, marble, granite, and of course a vast accumulation of calcareous organic remains ... I'm speaking from the English side of geology. What you will encounter at the Canadian end is for the Canadian geologists to work out.'

'Anything in the nature of volcanic seams?' Exmoor asked, thinking.

'It's possible, but we have no details at that depth. Only experience can show.'

'You'll be fighting the sea overhead, volcanic pressures, heat, fire-damp, the lot!' Lovelace said, his steel-trap mouth setting tightly. 'That's inevitable — but I believe you're the men with the sort of courage to fight such things.'

'And,' Schuster said, with a mental eye to finances, 'what is the payoff for all this drudgery, expense, and personal danger? Is it worth it all? Can it be repaid in pounds and dollars?'

Lovelace nodded in silent emphasis. 'In ten years, yes. There will be a handsome profit.'

'Ten years! A decade before we even start to get anything back! Perhaps not even then . . . '

'It will take at least ten years to bore our way. Our original estimate of cost is shown in your papers — but we may have to gamble on three times that much before we're through. We don't know what we'll run up against. Obviously, I can't carry a financial burden of that size alone. It would take the three of us all our time to do it. So we're going to advertise the scheme to the world when we've formed a Corporation and get in all the money we can. Since each one of us — Schuster, Brown and myself — is known to be financially sound I'll gamble on our being over-subscribed before we know it!'

'Perhaps,' Brown commented dubiously. 'I know plenty of the moneyed boys won't think there's much profit in a tunnel to Labrador! The aircraft and shipping companies will be against us all the way. They'll say we're planning to take a living out of their hands.'

Lovelace shrugged. 'Let them say so: they'll still be wrong. In this Bore there'll be a new type of railway, gentlemen — a monorail express. Instead of wheels it will have one huge ball bearing — or rather a series of ball bearings — which will fit into a special track. Speeds of up to four and five hundred miles an hour will be constantly maintained — a lightning service between this country and Canada.

Naturally we don't expect to achieve the speed of jet airliners, but on the other hand we shall not have to limit our loads as does the air traffic. And we'll be independent of all sea and air hazards, hurtling safely through the Bore whilst above there rages, perhaps, a winter tempest . . . That's only one advantage.'

Lovelace paused for a moment and then added, 'My friends, this is going to be a world affair before it's done, even if it is primarily controlled by the as yet hypothetical Bore Corporation. Everybody's going to benefit. In case of war there is a perfect pathway between the New World and the Old. In case of nuclear attack from above the Bore will still be safe because no nuclear bomb ever made can penetrate Steel-X. Power can even be obtained, if required, by draining selected portions of the seabed above us. Other advantages will occur to you, and believe me they are numerous. Trade will flow as never before. Even the United States can use the Bore — at a price. The profits, finally, will exceed the outlay. All we need to do is form the Corporation, issue a prospectus, and then watch the money roll in. The rest will be up to the engineers.'

Instinctively, because he knew the men he was dealing with, Lovelace knew he had won the hardest and most important part of the battle — that of getting the Bore Corporation formed. Even so, it took him nearly four hours, with only a hurried break for lunch, to get the answer he wanted. By the time he had finished answering questions, parrying difficult passages, and arguing for his point of view, even his inexhaustible energy was depleted.

It was just after four in the afternoon when the preliminary drafts referring to the intended Corporation were finished. Upon that point the meeting more or less broke up as far as the financial side was concerned — but Henry Saunders and his daughter, Exmoor, and Martin Astley remained in a tight circle to discuss the many preliminaries arising out of the copious notes made by geologist Gaulter. Lovelace hovered in the background, glad of a rest, but ready at any moment to answer any question. And presently one came — from Henry Saunders.

'I take it, Mr. Lovelace, that I now have the necessary carte blanche to go ahead on my own side of the Atlantic? Recruitment of labour, materials, and the general organization of the site?'

Lovelace nodded. 'Go right ahead. The Bore Corporation will back you on finance, and as you've seen from the draft proposals you're now Engineer-in-Charge, Canada.'

Saunders' huge chin expanded in a smile. 'I'm going to enjoy this job, D.L. I've always wanted something more than sinking deep shaft mines and artesian wells. Now it looks as though I've got it!'

Boyd Exmoor, who had been studying his own notes in silence, presently looked up to meet the tired eyes of Martin Astley.

'These drills you've designed, Mr. Astley, are unique.'

'Glad you think so,' Astley responded. 'I put a good deal of thought into them. You'll notice the Steel-X drills themselves are made in a variety of sizes, depending

25

on the type of stuff to be penetrated.'

Exmoor nodded and then pondered for a moment. A thought seemed to be troubling him.

'Anything wrong?' Lovelace asked, studying him.

'Only something that we ought to have cleared up. Where does all the excavated rubbish go to? It must be put somewhere.'

'There's a small fortune in the rubbish alone,' Lovelace reflected. 'We'll be digging up granite, marble, chalk, clay, and what-have-you. Apart from what we'll need for our own building contracts the surplus will be sold to building contractors who'll be damned glad to get it. Everything about this Bore will be productive. I've studied the angles very carefully.'

'My first moves,' Saunders said, taking a different tack, 'will be to get the labour and then delegate certain men whom I can trust to be foremen of their particular units, with myself in complete charge. I propose to gather together six labour corps with six men to oversee them. Each of the six will be in possession of plans duplicated from these originals, which I have here . . . My daughter will see to that,' he added, glancing at her.

'Willingly,' Judith Saunders agreed promptly, looking up. 'It may only be a small thing to do, but it will be my part in building the Bore. I've realized from the start what a wonderful feat of engineering this is going to be . . . Perhaps I've realized it even more than you men, who are mainly preoccupied with the financial and mechanical aspects. It's truly a magnificent dream, Mr. Lovelace!' the girl finished, with quiet earnestness.

'Thank you, my dear.' There was an odd, faraway look in Lovelace's eyes. 'I wish you were my daughter instead of Saunders'. All I've got is a son — and between ourselves he's nothing to be proud of.'

Nobody said anything. There was a conviction of embarrassment. None of those assembled, except Martin Astley, even knew that Douglas Lovelace had a son. Somehow, the men felt that they had been rather remiss in not praising

27

Lovelace for the idea he had launched. It had been left to this dark-haired girl with the intelligent grey eyes to do that. Exmoor, even now, felt he ought to say something, but he did not.

As a matter of fact he was not thinking about the Bore at the moment. He was remarking to himself what an attractive girl Judith Saunders really was. She had a knack of combining businesslike efficiency with feminine appeal. A rare gift. With a wry smile Exmoor reflected that it was perhaps unfortunate that she would be working on the Canadian side, some 3,000 miles away . . .

2

The troublemaker

The announcement of the formation of the Land's End-Labrador Bore Corporation and its aims hit the general public on both sides of the Atlantic with all the gentleness of an atom bomb, and it produced immediate results — both chaotic and otherwise. Naturally, the first to respond were the business men — the stockbrokers, bankers, the lesser known tycoons, the chain store millionaires — the whole brigade of them, amongst them many wealthy women too, who were intrigued by the idea of building a pathway under the inhospitable and tempestuous ocean.

Shares in the Corporation began to sell in tens, dozens, hundreds and then thousands. And associated with this came bigger deals of speculation in stone and metals, travel, railways, and transport generally. The little man and the big man were in this together, from a few hundred dollars and pounds to several million, depending upon the affluence of the buyer. On the British and Canadian stock exchanges brokers worked night and day — and when American big business smelled something lucrative the various operators on stocks and bonds nearly had a nervous breakdown keeping up with things.

Back in London, serenely calm in the midst of a worldwide net of confusion and vast agglomerations of finance, Douglas Lovelace surveyed the picture and was well pleased. Before even the first pick had been driven in the soil there was no longer any doubt about finances. His assessment of public and commercial reaction to the Land's End-Labrador Bore had been correct.

On the other hand, quite oblivious to the financial side but none the less girt up with overriding ambition, were Boyd Exmoor and Henry Saunders, opposite numbers in what was destined to be a race under the Atlantic. They alone, as they came gradually to realize, were the chief protagonists in this greatest of all earthly adventures about to commence . . . But, as yet, there was much to do. Both men were absorbed in the preliminary work of gathering together the labour necessary for the task. There were thousands of men to be housed and fed, their families to be kept in reasonable comfort, transport to be arranged for them, relaxation for their leisure hours to be studied.

On this side of the endeavour, Henry Saunders and his daughter worked with untiring energy in the inimical climate of Labrador. It was under their joint influence that they beheld a mushroom city grow between Zoar and Hopedale on the Labrador coast, a city designed to house the ever-growing army of workers — who in turn began the preliminary layout of the areas to form the Canadian end of the Bore.

Saunders was in constant contact by radio-telephone and closed-circuit television with Boyd Exmoor, who was also engaged in a tremendous labour task, and

31

without a staunch daughter to help him as Saunders had. But what he lacked in help he made up for in energy — a dynamic force equalled only by Douglas Lovelace himself. Exmoor wanted things done, and they were done, as fast and efficiently as humanly possible. In many ways, due to his great juniority of years compared to Saunders, he had an even greater driving force than his massive opposite number. Between them the two engineers, as they exchanged daily notes, cultivated a friendship of uncommon strength, a natural liking for each other and not a union just temporarily formed because they happened to be on the same project together. And at the westernmost tip of Land's End, perched high on that famous granite peninsula, there began to appear also the signs of a mushroom town, a town which overrode and devoured the existing dwellings around it, the inhabitants of which were moved at no expense to themselves, to other quarters inland. In the space of three months, thanks to furious work and building activity, the Land's End Peninsula was given over entirely to the Bore project, the demarcation line passing across from St. Ive's Bay to Mount's Bay, sealing off Cornwall proper. It was in the early spring the following year when both Saunders and Exmoor announced that they were ready to start. Television and movie screens, which had so faithfully mirrored progress to the world so far, now completed their task with a metaphorical burst of trumpets.

In the still winter-girt, icy climate of Labrador stood a small metropolis, and close beside it all the thousand and one engineering machines needed for the first plunge into hard Cambrian rock.

In Cornwall the scene was pretty much the same, save that the more tolerant climate gave a view of weak spring sunshine and shower-packed cloud piling up into a clear sky. Here, too, everything was ready to make the first strike into granite and Paleozoic rock. Predominant in both pictures, amidst an array of mining equipment, pithead-gear, and electrical apparatus for illuminating the site at night, stood six vast Astley borers — three to each project — all that had been manufactured so far. Over fifty feet high, with a projecting snout and drill of nearly a hundred feet — nuclear power engines in the rear of the wheeled structures — they resembled in some queer way prehistoric monsters, ready to jet flame and disintegration into whatever stood in their path.

On both sides of the Atlantic there was a ceremony of sorts, duly televised to the world, and then the job commenced! The two sites immediately became a bedlam of noise beside which the staccato rattling of a hundred pneumatic drills would have been sweetest music. The men themselves stood the racket because they wore plastic earplugs, specially designed for sound reduction. They knew it was an inevitable part of their job, so they worked on uncomplaining. But within a few days all those who lived just outside the mush-room towns quickly moved elsewhere. Day and night, ceaselessly, the row was something beyond human endurance.

To those who had the planning to do there was granted a modicum of peace. Both Saunders and Exmoor worked in sound-proofed offices — the headquarters of their particular site — overlooking the crazy array of mechanical navvies and busy labourers. On the English side, Exmoor studied the reports of progress supplied by his six 'generals' as the first excavations began. A huge crater a mile in diameter began to appear in the chalk and lime of Land's End, and from then on the hole grew deeper and fantastic structures pushed up against the skyline as props and underpinnings of Steel-X were manoeuvred into place.

Tracks were laid for the busy little railways that would carry the rubbish. Endless belt-conveyors were erected. More tracks were laid for the men to go back and forth. Tracks again for the mechanical navvies and grapnels to travel on as they nosed their way ever deeper into the earth and scooped out enormous mouthfuls of débris at every bite.

The job was going well. Only a fortnight had passed, and Exmoor was warily satisfied. So apparently, from his reports, was Henry Saunders. But of course the tough work had not even begun. This hell of noise and superhuman activity was only gardening compared to the task that lay ahead. Down, down, and still down man had to go — into black abysses under the seabed itself as yet never glimpsed or sounded by human beings.

Inevitably, even though the project had only just got under way, there were constant casualties. Sometimes they were caused mechanically, sometimes by rock falls, sometimes by lack of the necessary physique of some man to stand up to the gruelling work and screaming noise. A labour chief existed in both Land's End and Labrador — and in the Land's End department at least there was a raising of eyebrows by the labour boss as one of the prospective new recruits gave his name as Arthur Lovelace, university graduate son of Douglas Lovelace himself. Immediately Exmoor was contacted. In his own office he switched on the closed-circuit television and looked at the labour boss's face.

'What is it, Joe? Make it short.' Then Exmoor waited.

'There's a youngster here by the name

of Arthur Lovelace, boss. Son of old man Lovelace. What do I do? Recruit him?'

'Let me see him.'

At his own end the labour boss changed the buttons on his tele-transmitter. On Exmoor's screen the view shifted to that of a young man.

He was tall, well-built, and muscular, with a face something like his father. Except that Lovelace often smiled, whereas the son had the kind of face that didn't seem capable of humour.

'He looks all right,' Exmoor said, as the labour boss came in view again. 'I'll see if D.L. agrees. Hang on a moment.'

Exmoor reached to the telephone. Back in London Lovelace answered immediately on the private wire. Briefly Exmoor gave the circumstances.

'So that's where the young devil's got to!' Lovelace exclaimed. 'Can't imagine why he's turned his hand to labouring. Anyway, let him get on with it. Put him to work. I couldn't care less.'

'Couldn't care less?' Exmoor repeated, somewhat astonished at such lack of parental concern.

'That's what I said. Arthur's a dead loss as far as I'm concerned. I trained him at the university so he could get the full use of his intellectual powers — and he's got plenty! — and he rewards me by doing exactly as he likes, using my money, and following his own fancies. These fancies are not women, as you might suppose, but political groups. The lad's full of crazy ideas, so maybe a few months in the Bore will knock some of them out of him.'

'Right,' Exmoor said. 'We'll sign him on.'

So Lovelace junior was absorbed into the enormous, ever-growing labour army, and in spite of university degrees and attainments, in spite of his undoubted polish, he was at best nothing more than a labourer. He had chosen this menial work for some reason best known to himself and that was the end of it . . . or so it appeared.

The Bore progressed. In a month it had reached sea level from the top of the Land's End Peninsula. The excavators were driving through a conglomeration of clay, chalk and sand. As yet they had not come to tough rock — but they soon would according to the geologic tests constantly being made ahead of the activity. The ventilation system, comprised of a series of gigantic H-shaped shafts, was in the process of being constructed, ready to come into operation when the work finally plunged underground.

In Labrador the work against rock had really started. The geologic formation was such that rock layer began much sooner than in England, so the Astley borers were having their first real test — and standing up to it magnificently. Saunders was jubilant as he gave the details in his customary daily report.

'Tell Astley from me that he's a genius!' Saunders said, his big, craggy face filling the telescreen. 'There's nothing those drills can't go through! Have a look for yourself.'

The view switched. Exmoor found himself gazing at a couple of Astley borers, their projecting drills biting into the solid rock. Sparks and rock splinters were flying in all directions as the drills spun at an incredible number of revs per second. Even as Exmoor watched, a foot of progress was made into the solidity — then the view snapped back to Saunders again.

'Okay, I'll tell Astley the news,' Exmoor promised. 'He's a pretty immovable specimen, but I know he'll be glad underneath. You're doing nicely on your side . . . Here's ours.'

Exmoor switched the buttons, which, at the Canadian end, gave a view of British progress. Exmoor sat watching the scene in his monitor for a moment, then he resumed normal contact.

'And Judith, how's she making out?' he asked.

'Splendidly! I don't know what I'd do without her.'

Exmoor hoped — vainly — that the girl herself would appear on the screen, but Saunders evidently had no such ideas. His next words showed how far his daughter was from his immediate thoughts.

'We're going to beat you to the central rendezvous, Exmoor. I'm surprised that you haven't even started drilling rock yet. What the hell's the delay about? Six weeks, and this is as far as you've got! You'll have to start pulling your socks up, man. Don't you realize we've covered two miles?'

'You have?' Exmoor was astonished, but he did not show it. Instead he gave an easy grin. 'Don't start crowing too soon, Henry! We'll be at the central rendezvous long before you expect it even though we have got off to a slow start.'

'I'll wager we drill right through while you're still digging top soil,' the Canadian chaffed. ''bye for now. See you tomorrow.'

Exmoor returned the farewell and then faded out. He sat thinking for a moment, wondering if he could devise a feasible excuse for visiting Canada and renewing acquaintance with Judith Saunders at the same time. Then the girl drifted out of his mind again as he recalled something. The Canadians had travelled two miles whilst his own team had barely scratched the top surface. Something somewhere didn't add up.

The Bore, in the plans, was calculated

to sink diagonally and downward to a maximum depth of 2.5 miles, the British and Canadian ends being 1,250 miles each. And yet, after six weeks, a depth of only 1,000 feet or so had been reached on the British side whilst the Canadians had covered two miles. Exmoor was aware of a distinct hurt to his prowess as a mining engineer. In fact the job was taking far too long.

Annoyed, Exmoor deserted the quietness of his executive office and went to examine the site for himself, and so busy had he been until now it was actually his first visit to this mad world where half-stripped men, sweating and grimy, hurled all the modern forces of engineering against the adamant of Nature.

A small and powerful electric railway whirled Exmoor down to the 1,000-foot region where the searchlights blazed in profusion on the work in hand. The first thing that smote him was the din — smashing in from all sides. Behind him, as he alighted, the 1,000 feet of tunnel curved upwards and out of sight to the blessed surface and sunshine. Down here, three Astley drills were screaming their way into granite and gneiss rock, the first layer of which had at last been struck.

As fast as rock boulders were drilled or disintegrated, mechanical navvies went to work to shovel up the débris, depositing it in the trucks of waiting trains, which in turn lumbered and clanked their way up the curving ramp to the surface. With every foot now the task would get harder. Eventually the trains would have to cease because of the ever-increasing gradient, and conveyor belts would take their place.

Steel helmeted, perspiration wet on his face, Exmoor went over to the solitary foreman watching the proceedings. His eyes were on the drills driving into the rock, splitting it in sections. A narrow channel was cut in top and bottom of the rock face — the 'heading' process used in coal mines, by which method the removal of the rock was far simpler than trying to bore the whole mass.

'We're not making good time,' Exmoor shouted at length, and the foreman turned to look at him. Due to the noise he had not heard Exmoor's approach. He only knew now of his presence by the shouting so close to his ear.

'Best time we can,' the foreman answered. 'We daren't push things too much right now because we're under the sea for the first time, separated by only a thin layer from the Atlantic bed. If we strike too deep and too fast we'll have the ocean coming in.'

'What gave you that idea?' Exmoor snapped. 'You've seen the plans. If, as I assume, you're working to them exactly you'll not have any trouble. Or do you think we've been asleep in the executive offices?'

The foreman shrugged. 'Better safe than sorry, sir.'

'Look, we've got twelve hundred and fifty miles to go — through God knows what — and we've a specified time to do it in, a time dictated by money and resources,' Exmoor said. 'This is no way to get the job done. Maybe it's time we had an understanding . . . Stop the drills.'

'Stop the drills?' the foreman shouted, as the scream of Astley Steel-X on rock

44

split the airwaves.

'Now!' Exmoor ordered — and stood waiting.

The foreman gave a visual signal with his lamp — the only means of communication in the Babel — and in the distance another man gave a second signal. After a moment or two the drills stopped their awful clangour and the mechanical navvies ceased digging. Save for the relentless drip, drip, drip of water seeping, there was a deadly hush in this hole 1,000 feet down. Men stood waiting, removing the plastic stoppers from their ears. Some leaned on their tools. They stretched back up the curving ramp in their sweating, grim-faced thousands.

Exmoor pulled a small megaphone from the foreman's belt — an extra aid to his voice when visual contact was impossible — and then hurried over to one of the drills. From its high eminence he surveyed the grimy workers and they in turn surveyed him — sullen, strangely defiant, a mood that Exmoor found hard to understand.

'Now, men . . . ' He stood with his

hands on his hips, steel-helmeted head thrown back arrogantly. 'It's time we faced up to one or two things. First, we've only covered a little over a thousand feet, and it's taken us six weeks to do it. Canada has covered two miles in that time, with far greater difficulties to overcome. What's the matter with you? What the hell are you being so cautious about?'

'As I told you, Mr. Exmoor, we've got to be,' the foreman said. 'If we go too fast the sea will cave in on us.'

Exmoor eyed him. 'All the time you are moving forward, and as you move forward you go deeper and deeper, away from all risk of penetrating the sea bed. That danger, if any, existed only at the outset and is not operative now. We've got to cover one thousand two hundred and fifty miles. This crawl has got to stop from this moment. The plans are worked out so that danger from the seabed is remote — except in the case of bad workmanship, faulty direction, or accident.'

The men looked at each other but they did not say anything. Exmoor could still sense there was something in the air, and it was not his way to feel mystified if he could help it.

'This 'go slow' policy isn't natural,' he snapped. 'It's been operating since the beginning. Who's put you up to it?'

There was a shuffling of feet and some downcast eyes, but nobody answered.

'All right,' Exmoor said quietly. 'I can't replace the whole labour force, but if I could I would from this moment. I'll tell you this: because of the time you've lost I'm taking over the control of this section myself, and I'll see to it that you work like demons! You, Lacy,' — he looked at the foreman close beside him — 'will be transferred to M section.'

Lacy gave a start then abruptly he narrowed his eyes. 'The M section isn't nearly as important as this one, Mr. Exmoor, and not nearly so well paid.'

'I'm aware of it,' Exmoor retorted. 'The way you've handled your responsibility in this section makes you unworthy of anything better than the M section.'

'Look, I can do better than this — much better. Only — ' Lacy hesitated

47

as Exmoor's sharp eyes studied him. 'I've been listening to warnings, sir, the same as the rest of the boys, and that's made me uneasy.'

'Warnings? What the devil are you talking about? Can't you trust the plans and method of procedure given to you?'

'I suppose we ought to — but there's a mighty convincing argument on the other side. And from somebody who ought to know, too!'

'Who is it?' Exmoor snapped.

'Arthur Lovelace. Since he's the son of the boss he ought to know what he's talking about.'

'So that's it!' Exmoor gave a taut smile. 'I've known for some time there was a wrong element present — and I'll fix it, and quickly! All right, Lacy, I'll give you one more chance. Drive these men to the limit of speed and ignore everything except my own orders from here on. Right?'

'Right, sir — and thanks. I'll think of something to tell the men — to explain myself away, sort of. I suppose I've been a fool to listen to Lovelace along with the others but he has a mighty convincing way with him.'

'He won't have when I've finished with him . . . All right, get back to work!'

Exmoor stepped down from the drill, satisfied now that he had the solution to the problem that had bothered him. The shouting of Lacy's voice through the megaphone, as he explained the situation, together with the resumed scream of the drills, was enough for Exmoor. There would not be trouble again, not of that sort, anyway.

When he reached his office again he immediately contacted the five other men who were his immediate lieutenants in different sections of the enterprise. None of them, it appeared, had fallen under the spell of Arthur Lovelace — but then they hardly would since their particular jobs were not concerned with the actual drive through the rock. Their departments were associated with transport, provisions, shaft security, ventilation, and so forth.

'But why should Lovelace junior want to slow down his father's work?' Exmoor muttered to himself, tossing aside his steel helmet. 'It doesn't make sense — but it soon will.'

He snatched up the personnel telephone, gave the order for Arthur Lovelace to be found and sent to him, then he waited grimly through an interval, his eyes on the teeming industry of the site visible through the office window. Presently Arthur Lovelace arrived, steel-helmeted, shirt sleeves rolled up to the elbow on his young and powerful forearms. Exmoor surveyed him, assessing details that up to now he had only seen through the television screen.

Exmoor noted again the sardonic mouth, the general facial expression of intolerance, and the strongly packed young body. Arthur Lovelace might be an intellectual from his University training, but he was also a young Hercules to judge from his physique.

'I was told you wanted me, sir,' he said, looking at Exmoor as he stood by the window.

Exmoor turned and asked a blunt question. 'What's your grudge against the Bore, Lovelace?'

'Grudge?'

'Yes — grudge!' Exmoor's eyes had a hard look. 'You've been spreading discontent amongst the Bore men, warning them of all sorts of things that only exist in your imagination. Not a very good example to set as the son of the man who dreamed up the Bore, is it, Lovelace?'

The young man's face did not change expression. 'I can't help it if the fools took me seriously.'

'Fools, you say? Those men on the Bore are enduring constant strain, living in a world of hellish din, digging and boring like moles away from the sun and fresh air — and you call them fools. Time you got wise to yourself, isn't it, Lovelace?'

'I am wise to myself, sir. I know exactly what sort of conditions there are down here. I'm in them myself.'

'You're not working on the Bore itself. You're in transport.'

'The conditions are still rigorous, none the less. All I told the men was that they'd run into danger if they didn't use a bit of caution. I was only trying to protect their lives, and the interests of my father.'

Exmoor hesitated for a moment, then he came across from the window and looked at the young man squarely.

'You'll allow me to do the protecting in future, Mr. Lovelace, and you'll also remember that I'm the undisputed boss of this job. Maybe you acted from the best motives and maybe you didn't: I can't be sure. In future, whatever may be your personal opinion, keep it to yourself and don't influence the men. Understand?'

Lovelace nodded, his face as wooden and expressionless as ever.

'Otherwise you're finished,' Exmoor said. 'Now you can go.'

Lovelace gave a long stare of his grey eyes, then with something like a shrug he picked up his steel helmet from the chair where he had thrown it and left the office. From the window Exmoor watched him striding back towards the site, arrogance in every movement of his lithe young body.

'A Lovelace he might be,' Exmoor muttered to himself, 'but I don't like him.'

He wished for a moment that young

Lovelace had perpetrated some real crime, then he would have had an excuse for getting rid of him. As it was there was none — and to fire him without a legal reason would be difficult business, especially when it came to explaining things to D.L. himself.

Then, abruptly, Exmoor dismissed the worry from his mind. For the moment all was straight again and he had an enormous amount of work to do. He turned back to his desk and resumed his normal task of plotting, planning, and devising, pausing only now and again as the telephone rang and he transmitted some new instruction.

Certainly, his plain speaking to Lacy seemed to have an effect. From that moment onwards the Bore foreman was a changed man. He allowed neither let-up nor hindrance with his men, once he had explained things to them. They worked like demons, the giant Astley borers digging deeper and deeper downwards, throwing back an eternal deluge of débris and rock splinters, hazing the search-lighted enclosure with a dusty fog in the midst of which the men laboured like a vast army of grey phantoms.

As in the Land's End section, so in Labrador. The same hell of noise, the same frantic activity, the same gamble with the unknown. In another week Canada had moved on a further couple of miles: in Land's End all leeway had been made up so that both ends could report identical progress. After which, as far as Land's End was concerned, it was a matter of biting through solid granite. And even on this tough rock the Astley borers experienced no difficulty.

Work was going well. Exmoor and Saunders were both satisfied. When they had both covered twenty miles they declared a simultaneous day's holiday for the men — a pause in which the workers could go to the surface and enjoy something of normal life. A pause in which the eternal din was silenced. A pause in which the engineers responsible could survey at close quarters the progress made so far.

Exmoor spent the morning of the day's 'vacation' in company with Gaulter the geologist, Douglas Lovelace, and Martin Astley. All four men went down to the working site and silently surveyed the towering walls of neatly cut rock, the gleam of projecting mineral substances, and high above the spearing barbs of granite stalactites depending from the roof. Everything was clear and quiet in the glare of the everlasting searchlights.

'Mmm, favourable enough,' Lovelace commented at last, a steel helmet on his head and his steel-trap mouth as resolute as ever. 'The only thing I don't quite agree with is this day's holiday business. Don't forget we've a schedule to keep to. Twenty miles isn't much when we've got twelve hundred odd to cover.'

Exmoor shrugged. 'You can't work the men forever, D.L. A break like this will do them all the good in the world. The men engaged on the actual boring have the toughest job and they deserve the rest.'

'Up to you,' Lovelace said finally. 'I don't agree with it. Never take a holiday myself. There's time enough to rest when you're dead.'

'Before we're finished a lot of these

men will be,' Exmoor said quietly. 'I don't want any of them to say that the Bore project is nothing better than a forced labour camp. That could happen if certain people started to influence them.'

'What people, anyway?' There was an ominous look in D.L.'s eye.

'Your son, for one. He nearly tripped us up at the beginning with a go-slow policy. I nipped it in the bud and since then there's been no trouble.'

'And you kept Arthur on?' Lovelace demanded.

'Certainly. He'd committed no major crime. He's working on transport, and as far as I can check he's keeping his mouth shut.'

'See that he stays that way. I told you, didn't I, that he's got a head full of damned silly notions? If he causes any more trouble refer him to me. I'll deal with him.'

'Right, sir, I will.' Exmoor smiled with relief, glad that he had shifted some of the responsibility.

'Otherwise,' D.L. said, surveying, 'everything seems to be going all right. Those borers of yours are a masterpiece, Martin. Think of trying to pierce this lot with normal drills. The damned things would have been chewed to blazes by now.'

'When we get something too tough for Steel-X we'll have to give up,' Astley said, scooping the untidy hair from under his steel helmet. 'I'll guarantee they'll carry us all the way to the central rendezvous.'

Lovelace turned to go, then he stopped. His eyes were on an array of a dozen lamps perched at different angles on the deserted rock face where, on the morrow, drilling would resume. Each lamp was high up and glowed with a solemn yellow light all its own.

'Fire damp lamps,' Exmoor explained, following Lovelace's gaze. 'Just in case of trouble. They're an improved version of Sir Humphrey Davy's mining lamps. In the event of any fire damp gas seeping through the rock face they'll turn blue.'

'Who'll see them, anyway?' Astley questioned, looking about him.

Exmoor nodded to a mass of steel galleries further back along the tunnel.

'There's a skeleton staff up there,

always on duty — even on a holiday like this. They're the Protection Squad. They can see right away if fire damp is showing itself and take measures to stop it, or seal off the section where it's occurring. They also have sensitive instruments for instantly recording the presence of carbonic acid, carbon monoxide, or any other kind of gas that might be prevalent at these depths. Because all of these gases are lighter than air they rise to the roof — hence the height of the Protection Squad's headquarters. Those headquarters move along with the men as they bore deeper.'

'Good work,' Lovelace complimented. 'Leave nothing to chance.'

Exmoor said nothing. He did not consider it necessary to explain to Lovelace the thousand and one things that were in operation for the safety of the men — and the project. Lovelace was a financial genius, and a great organizer, but his knowledge of mine engineering could be encompassed on a thumbnail and still leave room to spare.

Gradually, still surveying as they went,

the men returned to the fussy little train waiting to take them back up the ramp to the surface. They had a distance of a mile to walk through the huge underground workings. The railway track did not extend this far. Already the steep upward climb was proving too much for normal traction. Silent conveyor belt systems spanned the length of the brilliantly lit tunnel on each side.

As the train came within view Lovelace stopped for a moment and looked back. He clapped his hands together in sudden ecstasy and one of those rare smiles broke on his tough, resolute face.

'Can't you just picture it, boys, when all this is completed, say in ten years from now?' His arms went unexpectedly about the shoulders of Exmoor and Astley as they stood on either side of him. 'This great Bore, lined with its beautiful Steel-X, and with the nuclear energy lamps gleaming overhead with the brightness of day? Think too of the pedestrian tracks, stretching for two thousand five hundred miles alongside the Bore walls, with the small rest centres every ten miles for the walkers to stay and rest or relax. Imagine too the motorways higher up than the pedestrian ways. And in the centre, a racing demon of power and speed, will be the track of the Cannonball Express. It's a vision to delight the imagination and the mind.'

'Cannonball Express?' Exmoor repeated, surprised.

'Surely — my monorail idea. Its main motive power is from a series of giant balls instead of wheels — Steel-X balls that will withstand a lifetime of wear and friction.'

'Hmmm,' Exmoor acknowledged, with a nod of admiration. 'I like that name quite a lot. Sounds — er — powerful, suggestive of accomplishment and things done.'

'But before they are done there's the hell of a lot to conquer,' said the geologist pensively. 'Far be it from me to be a wet blanket, but up to now you've had only a picnic. When you get into the real depths — into the hundreds of miles — you'll really be up against it.'

'We'll get through,' Lovelace said

confidently, turning to continue the walk to the waiting train. 'Man has never failed yet in his conquest of Nature, and he won't this time.'

In a few more minutes they reached the train and were quickly transferred to the surface. Exmoor took his leave of Lovelace and Gaulter checked a few notes with Martin Astley, and then headed for his office. He was thinking of a variety of problems as he entered it — but they went out of his mind as he suddenly realized he had a visitor, seated waiting at the desk.

It was Judith Saunders.

3

Deadly explosion

'Why, Judith!' Exmoor whipped off his steel helmet and hurried over to where the girl was seated, neatly attired in a summery suit of light grey. 'When on earth did you get here, and why didn't you tell me you were coming?'

She returned his handshake warmly and then smiled as he sat beside her.

'It was a snap decision, really. Dad said it was about time we had some more duplicate plans from your end — as well as a discussion on progress. In fact quite a lot of things that couldn't be done by television. So, since he doesn't want to stray far from the fold in case he's needed I volunteered to take advantage of the day's holiday and fly over. I left Canada about eight this morning.'

'And arrived to find me missing,' Exmoor said in regret.

'Don't worry. Your site-keeper at the gates told me you'd gone below with Mr. Lovelace and the others. I knew you wouldn't be long.'

Exmoor smiled. He was reflecting that Judith looked just the same, with her pretty face, grey eyes, and dark hair. It didn't seem to occur to him that there was no reason for her to be any different.

'Er — you said a discussion on progress?' he asked.

'That's right.' Judith nodded to her briefcase on the desk. 'Dad wants Plans Number 19 and 26, and a full duplicated copy of your geologic findings to date. Just to check with his own records.'

'I could have sent them to you,' Exmoor said, and at that Judith glanced downwards shyly.

'I suppose you could — but I believe in the personal touch.'

'Hmmm, yes. Nothing like it.' Exmoor was silent for a moment and then glanced at his watch. 'The discussion can come later, can't it? It's only eleven o'clock as yet.'

'Yes, I suppose it could.' The level grey

eyes studied him.

'I was just thinking — I'm entitled to a holiday as much as anybody else, particularly so now there's somebody who'll enjoy it with me. At least I hope you will. Care to have lunch with me if we hop over to London away from this confounded site for a while?'

'I'd love it!'

Decision became reality. At top speed Exmoor changed into a lounge suit, then escorted the girl out to his fast car. In a little under ninety minutes, following the new fast coast road, they were in London. Exmoor selected the restaurant, one that he knew from experience was ideal, and for the time being he did his best to forget that he was boss of a gang of human moles and concentrated on the girl instead.

Inevitably, though, conversation presently drifted round to the Bore.

'You're satisfied with progress, Mr. Exmoor?' the girl asked, when the lunch had arrived.

'By and large, yes. Even though I am warned by our geologist that the worst has yet to come.'

'Only to be expected. No great dream was ever realized without its attendant setbacks and heartaches.' Judith ate daintily as she made this observation. 'Dad, too, knows that the present progress is too ridiculously easy to be maintained . . . But, whatever happens, it will be worth it in the end, don't you think?'

'Entirely worth it, yes.' Exmoor shifted position slightly. 'I'd rather hoped that we could forget the Bore for a while, Miss Saunders.'

'Oh? Why? Isn't it the one thing we're interested in?'

'Of course, but there are other things, you know. Remember the old saying about all work and no play . . . ?'

Judith was silent, but she gave a glance of her grey eyes. Womanlike, she left Exmoor — never a brilliant conversationalist unless he was on the topic of engineering — to sort out the mess he had himself precipitated.

'I don't believe,' he said, with sudden firmness, 'that you made the airtrip from

Canada solely to discuss details which could have been taken care of electronically. You certainly don't need to view the progress we've made because that's been televised as well. As for the plans you want for your father they could — as I said earlier — have been sent to you.'

Judith laughed softly. 'From all of which, what conclusion do you draw, Mr. Exmoor?'

'Well — er — it may sound egotistical, but I can only think that you came to see me — personally, and not as a matter of business.'

'Yes — you're quite right,' Judith said frankly. 'Where's the sense in wrapping it up. I suppose I've got a bit of nerve really, only I thought I'd like to get better acquainted with the man who's boring his way from the other side of the Atlantic.'

Exmoor's doggedly earnest face expanded in a wide grin.

'Well, Madam, here I am — a lonely engineer filled with tons of ambition, but in the unfortunate position that I've nobody to share it with — like you have with your father.'

'I don't share very much with him,' Judith sighed. 'We're good pals of course, and get on famously together on this Bore business, but otherwise we're not particularly interested in each others' pursuits. After all, what does a bright young maiden of twenty-five want for fishing?'

'Fishing?'

'Why, yes! That's dad's only hobby — and he expects me to keep him company. I do so to please him but honestly — ! You're not a spare time fisherman, are you?'

'No,' Exmoor grinned. 'My problem is to find the spare time. But joking apart, I'm flattered that you've sought me out. I've tried to contact you on several occasions, via TV, since we first met at Lovelace's original meeting but I've always been unlucky. I've asked after you a lot; did your dad tell you?'

'Yes — in an offhand sort of way. I realized that you would never have inquired after me had you not been interested, so I decided at the first opportunity to fly across and have a chat with you.'

From that moment the ice was broken. Between them, the two covered an enormous amount of ground in what was left of the day. After lunch they strolled around London in the warm sunshine, rested in Regent's Park, and all the time — precious time — they got to know all about each other. Their interests were kindred, they laughed at the same things, and were determined on the same issues. To Exmoor it was heaven, and he hoped it was the same for the girl. When at last, in the late evening, they got back to Exmoor's office on the Land's End site they each felt as though they had known each other from childhood.

Silently, for he had practically run out of words, Exmoor handed the girl the two plans she required and a copy of the geologic findings to date, then he stood watching her as she put them in her briefcase.

Finally she was finished. She snapped the catches and picked the case up.

'Well, Boyd — back to the grindstone,' she said cheerfully. 'Thanks for a lovely day. Thanks again and again.'

'It cuts both ways,' he said, taking her slender hand in his own big ones as she extended it. 'I was interested in the Bore before, as you know — but now I'll go to town with a vengeance. I'll think all the time that there's somebody on the other side of the Atlantic waiting for me to get through.'

'And I'll egg father on and hurry him up,' she laughed. 'The Bore will be finished before we know it . . . Don't look so glum!' she reproved suddenly. 'There'll be other holidays — other days. We'll make an opportunity to see each other even if it's only on the pretext of attending to business.'

'Of course . . . ' Exmoor held her hand tightly, then as her face came nearer, whether unintentionally or deliberately he did not know, he kissed her warmly. She smiled but did not say anything as he suddenly released her.

'The plane won't wait,' she said seriously, with a glance at her watch.

'Lord, no! I'd forgotten all about it.'

Exmoor did not waste any more time. He whirled the laughing girl out to his car and made the journey to the airport in record time. His last awareness of her was her hurried farewell kiss and the steady climb of the strato-cruiser into the sky. Exmoor watched it until the evening swallowed it up and the scream of the jets had died into silence.

Only then did he turn back to his car. He had a great deal to think about — pleasant things, warm, human things that had nothing to do with the merciless granite and hellish noise of the Bore. It surprised him to realize that he was in love. His forthright, tough-hitting disposition did not accept the fact easily. But there it was . . . Judith Saunders represented to him all that was beautiful and sincere in life.

★ ★ ★

The next morning Exmoor was back on the job — but with a song in his heart. An early telecall from Canada had revealed the fact that Judith had arrived home safely and her father was satisfied with the plans and findings she had brought. For the moment that was all. Ahead was work — work — and more work.

Through his office window Exmoor watched the labourers arrive for the first shift, then presently the drills started up. The mechanical navvies followed suit, and within fifteen minutes all the old Babel of noise and furious energy had returned. Exmoor smiled wryly to himself and settled down to his usual task of planning one jump ahead for the struggling men.

It was around 10:15 when something happened, and it first registered on Exmoor, busy at his desk, as a confused kind of shouting. He looked up in puzzled interest, and at the same moment there smote on his ears the frantic blaring of the alarm siren, piercing rough the chaos of noise outside.

Immediately Exmoor dived to the window. There smote upon him vision of scurrying men, falling over obstacles in their frantic desire to escape from the main site of operations. In the distance the drills were still boring, but they seemed to be unattended. Everywhere men were running as though from the Devil himself. Exmoor's eyes rose to the safety lamps, and suddenly he knew what was the matter. The lamps had turned blue — a sure sign of toxic and explosive gas.

Instantly he swung, diving for the phone that contacted with the Protection Squad. But he never reached it. He was halfway across the office when a vast concussion belched from outside. The office rocked. Swaying on his feet Exmoor had a glimpse of men flying through the air like leaves in a gale. A forked tongue of flame shot from high up in the rock face, blasting away the safety lamps. An immense shock wave brought down underpinning and props, overturned the drills, and uprooted the heavy navvies. Men, hundreds of them, vanished in a crazy smother of rocks, soil, and débris.

The lights went out as the searchlights overturned. Exmoor was in blackness, the office still shuddering — but gradually it ceased and things were quiet again. He groped his way round to the desk and picked up the phone.

'Exmoor here,' he said tensely. 'Anybody listening?'

There was a long pause before a hoarse, shaken voice answered.

'Protection Squad speaking . . . '

'Who's talking?' Exmoor demanded.

'Benson, sir. The others seem to be knocked out, or else dead. I can't tell. There's no light.'

'I know that. Try your alarm system to the surface. Set it going. Get the rescue squad here right away.'

'Yes, sir — ' Out of the unholy quiet and darkness there came a sudden penetrating wail, of a different note to the one that had warned of gas. It was actually the call for help, and with its wailing a dozen similar sirens went into operation, radio controlled, on the surface. Immediately a ready-and-waiting gang of rescuers would come to investigate.

'I've — I've sounded it, sir,' came Benson's shaky voice.

'I can hear it. Do what you can to revive your comrades and leave the rest to me. I'm going to try the emergency lighting.'

73

Exmoor slammed the 'phone back onto its rest, then darted over to the big switchboard at the rear of his office. Nearly all switches to deal with an emergency were under his control, including that of lighting. In a matter of moments he had killed the juice on the main cable to the smashed searchlights and switched in a secondary lighting system, running from batteries instead of the generators that had location on the surface. Through the office window a yellow glow came into being, beaming through the haze of settling dust.

Exmoor gave a grim sigh as he surveyed the chaos. Then he snatched up his steel helmet and hurtled outside. Coughing in the evil-smelling haze he stumbled over rocks and overturned machines, until he had a clearer view of the disaster. There were mangled and half buried men everywhere and the machinery was either smashed or up-ended. There was only one bright spot in the situation: the gas did not seem to be issuing any more. Evidently the whole pocket of it had blown off at once — and with devastating force.

Sounds made Exmoor glance round. Those men who had escaped vere returning now, cautiously, ready to dive backwards at the first sign of trouble. Behind them the tunnel extended, dusty and foggy. Fortunately the way to the surface was clear.

One of the men reached Exmoor at last and looked at him with troubled eyes.

'How bad is it, boss?'

'Bad enough, but it could have been a lot worse. I can't figure out how it happened with no naked light and no smoking. There'll have to be an inquiry . . .' Exmoor looked back at the men climbing over the rocks. 'All right, you men, give me a hand. We'll do what we can until the rescue team arrives.'

★ ★ ★

For the time being the British end of the Bore was at a standstill. It took all the remainder of the day, with the survivors, rescue teams, and men of the other divisions working at full pressure to

75

extricate the dead and injured and put the overturned machines on normal balance. A count-up revealed that there were 270 men dead and 42 injured. As far as the machinery was concerned there was no damage that could not be repaired. The navvies had suffered the worst. The Astley drills, on the other hand — most valuable equipment of all — had not even been dented.

The next day the work resumed, but there was no doubt of the fact that the men were unnerved. Up on the surface, in homes where workers would never return, there was grief and growing discontent. This was the first time that real tragedy had struck, and although everybody had known that it must come some day, that did not make it any the more palatable. There began a hint-and-whisper campaign amongst the bereaved. Was the Bore really worth it?

Exmoor shut his ears to all the talking, even though he knew it was there. First he had to face an inquiry in London, the upshot of which amounted to precisely nothing. There was no answer for the disaster, and he for his part had taken all the necessary steps to put things right. The answer seemed to be that somehow a naked light, a spark, or something unlooked-for had ignited the fire-damp gas — but with every precaution taken and no man allowed to smoke how had trouble arisen?

No solution — at present. Exmoor was instructed to draft in 270 more men and spend what time he could in trying to locate the cause of the blow-out. He returned to his office, gave his orders to the labour recruitment boss, and then continued work as usual. There was nothing much else that he could do.

It was foreman Lacy, who had escaped the fire-damp explosion, who finally provided — nearly a week later — a possible answer for the tragedy, and he made his statement as though he were half afraid of it. Coming into Exmoor's office in a mid-afternoon shift he said bluntly:

'I've been thinking, sir — about that fire-damp business. It might have been young Lovelace again.'

Exmoor stared. 'Lovelace! What the devil gave you that idea?'

'Well, sir, just before the blow-out, he brought a truck full of small tools down to the rockface where we were working . . .'

'And?'

'When he'd unloaded the tools he started the truck up again and deliberately caused a backfire. Anyway, I think it was deliberate. I saw the flame shoot from the truck's exhaust pipe. I was going to warn him about it but the explosion came immediately afterwards. I saw the truck up-end and heel over with the blast, but I'd like to gamble it was Lovelace's crazy action that caused the disaster.'

Exmoor was silent, his face grim. Lacy shifted uncomfortably.

'I'd have mentioned it sooner, but I only just happened to remember it.'

Exmoor said: 'Rightly or wrongly there's not much we can do about it. Lovelace is in the Transport department, of course, and a backfire could happen to anybody. It's difficult to credit that he would do such a thing deliberately. He wouldn't know fire-damp gas was about.'

'He might if he happened to see the emergency lamps turning blue, sir.'

'Even granting that possibility the explosion could have killed him as much as anybody else.'

'But it didn't!' Lacy argued. 'All he got was a bruised arm. The back of the truck and the cabin round the driver's seat protected him. He was back at work in a couple of days.'

Exmoor shook his head. 'Nothing I can do about it, Lacy. Not on such flimsy evidence. It's a possible answer but I can't think of it as deliberate.'

'You're the boss.' Lacy moved to the door; then he turned and looked back. 'I don't feel at all safe with Lovelace around, sir. I know he's the boss's son, but I'm convinced he's up to something, something which he believes is worth sacrificing his life for.'

Lacy went on his way, and for a moment or two Exmoor sat thinking. He realized the foreman could conceivably be right — that Lovelace junior had some kind of axe to grind. It was even possible that he had noticed the lamps turning blue, and with extraordinary adroitness of thought had created a brief flame in the form of a backfire. But why? What on earth had he taken such a stupendous risk for, which could well have involved his own life?

Exmoor sighed. Possibilities — and nothing more. He could not tackle Lovelace about the matter for there was nothing to go on, but he could, and would, have him watched carefully from this moment onwards. If Arthur Lovelace was really determined to hinder the Bore effort he would try something else before long — and walk right into a trap.

Exmoor picked up the telephone and switched through to the squad of men who acted as personnel detectives. Roby, the head man, answered.

'I've a job for you, Roby,' Exmoor said. 'Detail a couple of men to keep a constant eye on Arthur Lovelace, of Transport. The boss's son. I suspect him of quite a few things, but I've nothing concrete. If he steps out of line in the smallest particular arrest him — And have your men look like transport workers to prevent suspicion attaching to them.'

'Right, Mr. Exmoor. I'll see to it.' Exmoor rang off and turned back to his work. With the problem delegated to men who could watch the situation carefully he felt he had done all that was needful. If Arthur Lovelace was a genuine enemy of the Bore he would trip himself up sooner or later . . .

The work went on. The blowout was forgotten — or almost. It had an echo in that there was considerable difficulty in getting new men to take the place of those who had died. Men were not anxious to volunteer for the Bore when they knew that 270 had been wiped out. So the Labour Recruitment Department fell back on 100 Europeans to supplement the 170 Englishmen already signed on. Foreign labour was at work, but at least they were tough and seemed willing, and that was the main thing. Exmoor himself did not quite like the idea, but he had no choice. His only concern was to bore — bore — and bore.

The twenty miles of progress became

twenty-five — thirty — forty miles, and all was going well. As fast as the invincible drills bored through the virgin rock, teams came up in the rear to line the gleaming walls with huge sheets of Steel-X, which in turn were carried up in arching sections to the roof. Then the sections were sealed together with liquid Steel-X hardening to unimaginable toughness. This was a process that Martin Astley constantly supervised himself. No ordinary welding could possibly compare with this system of bonding, a system that relied basically on the terrific heat of nuclear power.

Men worked ceaselessly on the welding process — goggled, sweating men in a temperature of a hundred Fahrenheit degrees, holding out before them the blinding, searing jets that made the fusion possible. Beyond them again, pressing ever forward, were the huge drills with their indescribable clamour. Less conspicuous, but still vitally important, were the ever-full conveyor belts moving débris up forty miles of shaft to the surface.

Behind the army of bore-controllers, welders, conveyor men, and transport armies, came the team engaged on the ventilating system — and marching hand-in-hand with them were the Protection men in their mammoth, moveable dwellings, always on the look-out for trouble, keeping a day and night watch over their instruments and seismographs. They were alert for the merest quiver of the earth that might presage disaster. After the blow out they were doubly watchful.

It was only as the project advanced that Exmoor realized the enormity of it. Progress had carried them forward 40 miles and to a depth of 2,500 feet. At every mile they were separated from the still shelving bed of the Atlantic Ocean by a barrier of rock 500 feet thick — and that barrier width had always to be maintained right up to the central rendezvous. Even so, the danger would mount as the pressure increased under the weight of waters above. Whatever danger there was — if any at all — was in the future, and Exmoor was forced to leave it at that.

Time and again, as things progressed,

Exmoor contacted Canada and exchanged information. Several times he spoke to Judith herself, but though both of them had the wish to exchange endearments they were also conscious that they would be out of place on the Corporation's television hook-up. So they confined themselves to business. And Saunders, although he knew of the attachment his daughter and Exmoor had for each other, never referred to it. He asked only for — and gave — progress reports.

In general, Canada seemed to be keeping up with Britain, though it appeared that they were two miles behind in the advance. Their total boring amounted to 38 miles against Britain's 40.

'Who'll have to start pulling his socks up now?' Exmoor asked drily, when he heard the news. 'We lost a day through that blow-out and yet we're two miles ahead of you. What's your trouble? Losing your enthusiasm?'

'Anything but! We've struck a patch of rock that's harder than all hell. I'm half afraid that the drills will crack under it, but they don't. Once we're through we'll catch up and leave you standing.'

'You hope,' Exmoor grinned. 'Okay, Henry, I'll see you again tomorrow.'

'With ten miles in hand,' the Canadian warned, smiling; and then switched off. For a moment or two, in his own headquarters on the Labrador side, he sat pondering and rubbing his big chin.

'Anything the matter, dad?' Judith asked him presently, looking up from the plans she was checking.

'Matter? Not really . . . ' Saunders got up, considered some more, and then said: 'I just don't like the idea of Boyd Exmoor getting ahead of me.' And as Judith gazed in surprise he added, 'Oh, there's nothing personal in it. Just friendly rivalry. I want to beat him to that central rendezvous, and I don't care what means I use to do it.'

'Within reason, I hope?' Judith asked anxiously.

'Naturally.' Saunders picked up the phone and contacted the site. 'How's things down there, Sid? Making any progress?'

'Not the slightest,' Sid's voice responded. 'I've just got the geologist's report on the stuff we're trying to penetrate and it seems to be a conglomeration of pure carbon and tungsten together, both them under enormous pressure. I don't have to tell you that pure carbon is the same as the diamond, and rates Number 10 in Mohs' Scale of Hardness. Tungsten is rare in the raw state, of course, and there's hardly any on the surface, but here we've got a complete seam of it mixed with the carbon. How the devil we're going to get through it I don't know.'

'The drills won't take it?' Saunders asked.

'Not even slowly. They don't break, but this is like trying to smash through plate glass with a pin. The drill's power engines simply stall.'

'Have you tried a way round the barrier?'

'No use, sir. We'd have a ten mile detour, according to the geology boys.'

'I'll come down,' Saunders said. 'There's got to be a way somehow.'

Saunders put the phone down, looking into distance. Judith dropped her work and came towards him.

'What's the trouble, dad? I only heard one side of it.'

'We're up against carbon and tungsten under great pressure, Judy. The drills just cough back. I'm going down to see what I can do . . . ' Saunders picked up his steel helmet. 'Seems to me there's only one thing for it — blasting.'

A shade of alarm passed over Judith's face. She caught her father's arm as he moved towards the door.

'There's danger in doing that, dad. We can't be sure which way the blast stress will go. If it goes parallel we'll be all right, but if it strikes upwards it might shatter the five hundred foot barrier to the ocean. Then where will we be?'

Saunders hesitated. 'You seem to know a lot about this, Judy.'

'Why shouldn't I? I'm a mining engineer too, remember. It's my firm belief that blasting isn't the answer. We ought to cut round the obstacle.'

'That'd be at least ten miles, and think of the delay in a ten mile detour. Then there'd be another ten miles in getting back to the straight again. Hell, no.

87

There's got to be a quicker way than that.'

'It would only take a few months, and at least it would be safer,' Judith argued, but her father shook his head.

'Not for me, Judy. You forget I've got Boyd Exmoor watching my progress. I'm not going to fall behind for any damned barrier of carbon and tungsten.'

'Dad! That's just silly pride and it endangers all the — '

Judith said no more. Her father had departed. She shook her head moodily and went back to her work, but at best her efforts were only a pretence. She knew her father's determined and often impulsive nature, and yet she had no authority to dictate to him. Her job was to wait — and see what happened.

In the meantime Saunders was descending the great shaft in moody silence. Though he had not shown it, Judy's words had had a good deal of effect. He knew she was right: but on the other hand there was no reason why, correctly placed, blasting should not smash away the barrier. True, it would be the first time nuclear demolition had been tried at this depth, but there had to be a first time for anything. Nibbling at the problem was not Henry Saunders' way. He always went straight forward, with all the smashing power he could make available.

Presently he arrived at the curiously quiet site of operations to find the engineers lounging against their useless Astley drills, while Sid Ingrams himself was in consultation with the geological team around a portable table. It was covered with maps and figures.

'Well?' Saunders demanded, coming up in the searchlights' glare. 'Any nearer, boys?'

'Not a scrap,' Sid answered. 'We've tried the drills on needle smallness but they still won't bite. Either we detour by ten miles and redraft our progress, or else we try and blast our way through.'

Saunders did not answer immediately. He went over to the barrier and examined it minutely. Sid Ingrams stood by his side, waiting for observations.

'We'll blast,' Saunders decided finally. 'And for a very good reason. This barrier is worth something — worth millions on millions of dollars once it's removed to the surface and properly treated. Raw diamond, and nothing else but — and the tungsten is of high value because there's so little of it in the normal way. If we cut round the barrier and allow it to defy us we'll get nothing from it and lose an enormous amount of time. So we're going through! What do you boys think of the chances of a nuclear blowup?'

The geologists, thus addressed, looked at each other. Then one of them answered.

'Hard to say, Mr. Saunders. We've had no experience of nuclear explosions at a great depth: we can't estimate where the strain will come.'

'In other words you'd rather not commit yourselves?'

'We can't,' the geologist said frankly.

Saunders looked at Sid Ingrams. 'Detail the necessary men to fix the smallest nuclear explosives at the bottom of the barrier then when they're fused up sound the alarm bell. The shaft will have to be cleared until the explosion's passed.'

'Right, sir.'

Ingrams went into action. Saunders stood grimly silent and watched as the explosives team went to work. In all they lined up four of the smallest-sized nuclear charges, linked them so they would fire simultaneously, and then they moved back up the shaft, taking with them the radio equipment with which they would fire the charges when required. The alarm sirens sounded and, as rapidly as convenient, the shaft was emptied of men, all of them going up to the surface where there was no danger of fallout.

The job took some hours. Saunders himself saying little but watching everything. He was one of the last to leave, and it was his task to give the order for firing.

In the gathering gloom of the evening he looked about him at the immense shaft top, at the hundreds of men waiting expectantly for results — and finally at the engineers grouped around their radio-firing equipment. Over at the executive offices — fully aware by now of what was going on, Judith waited in tense anxiety.

'Right!' Saunders said abruptly. 'Fire!'

The engineer-in-charge pressed a switch. For a second or two nothing seemed to happen. Nothing was changed in the glare of arclight . . . Then from the depths there came a muttering growl, a shivering grumble that made the ground quake. The vast assembly of men waited tensely for worse to come — but nothing more happened. And nothing seemed any different. Very slowly Saunders expelled a sigh of relief.

'How long before we can venture down, boys?' he asked the engineers.

'Right now, sir, wearing insulated suits. Fallout will be pretty heavy at the moment.'

'Okay. Get me a suit.' Saunders gestured quickly. 'I'm not asking for volunteers on this. I'll do it myself.'

Within ten minutes Saunders was duly inside his suit. He operated one of the lift shafts himself and began to descend, a powerful lamp blazing from his helmet. The lower he went the denser became the fog and dust and discharge from the explosion, but nothing happened to impede his progress to the bottom. Then at last the elevator reached the limit and he slammed back the gates and stood staring at the view.

The way was clear! The barrier of carbon-tungsten had ceased to exist and now lay about the site of operations in so many vast chunks and boulders, like a vast slab of coal that has been hit squarely in the middle.

Grinning triumphantly to himself behind his vizor, Saunders picked his way forward. There was plenty of débris to clear, of course, but that wouldn't take long. The point was that the barrier had gone and rock face loomed ahead, of which the drills would make short work.

Saunders reached the point finally where the barrier had been and stood looking about him. The roof had been exploded away, but not to a serious distance. And all around were these fabulous lumps of black streaked with grey, each worth a fortune when transported to the surface.

Saunders looked at his feet. The rock ground, which had received the full force of the nuclear impact, seemed curiously spongy under his rubbered and insulated boots. *Too* spongy!

He stepped back in sudden alarm, and he went to his knees in a rocky quicksand. He shouted soundlessly behind his vizor, then he was plunging downwards into blackness, hurtling into a vastly deep underground ravine, the shell of a shaft floor raining in after him. Three thousand feet below Saunders struck bottom.

4

The wall of gold

Not only the area through which Henry Saunders had plunged to his death was found to be friable, but everything on the ground within a mile area was in the same condition. Engineers, coming to investigate, discovered the tragedy — and the danger — beholding Saunders' dead body in the glare of a searchlight as it lay, a mere speck, 3,000 feet down.

It was decided to leave him there, in a grave deeper than any vouchsafed to man before. The danger area was covered with a solid floor of Steel-X five feet thick, supported and imbedded in the rock surrounding the weak area. Then work resumed, but Henry Saunders was remembered by a Steel-X plaque fashioned in the wall itself at the point where he had died. This particular position of the Bore would be known as Saunders

Crisis ever afterwards.

The whole world soon knew about the death of Saunders. Judith knew of it almost immediately, and Boyd Exmoor half an hour later. The shock had to be assimilated. Sid Ingrams had, for the moment, to take over the Canadian control until the Corporation decided what was to be done. Meanwhile the juggernaut progress of the Bore continued. The débris of the barrier was removed to the surface and the Bore Corporation silently congratulated itself on the acquisition of a sizeable fortune m diamonds and tungsten.

At the first opportunity, Exmoor deserted his post at the British end of the project and flew to Canada to get the facts of Saunders' death first hand from Judith. He found her in a deluge of work, handling her late father's and her own work, an effort which did much to stifle the grief that otherwise might have weighed her down.

Exmoor discovered her entirely cooperative, but obviously overworked.

'What happens now, Judy?' he asked,

when their first emotions at meeting again were over. 'How's this going to affect the project, do you think?'

The girl seated herself at the large desk. Her grey eyes looked unusually big and tired.

'I think there's only one answer,' she said finally.

'That Sid Ingrams will take over control?'

'No. He's not an accredited mining engineer. There's only one chief for the Canadian side, and that's me.'

Exmoor gave a start. 'You! But — '

'I know what you're thinking, Boyd. I'm a woman, and a woman digging a tunnel to England has never been heard of.'

'A woman digging a tunnel anywhere hasn't been heard of. Is that the decision of the Corporation or just a pipe dream of your own?'

Judith put her elbows on the desk and cupped her chin in her locked hands. She looked at Exmoor thoughtfully.

'I don't think the Corporation has any choice, Boyd, for the simple reason that I was dad's right hand. I knew everything he did, everything he intended to do. Nobody knows more about the Canadian end of this project than I do. Maybe I shan't move as fast as dad because I just won't take risks like he did, but I'll still meet you at the central rendezvous in the end.'

Exmoor gave a little, incredulous smile. 'I'm sure you will, Judy, but — Well, I just can't imagine you at the head of an enterprise as big as this.'

Judith sighed and got to her feet. She wandered over to the window and gazed out on the busy scene. She spoke half to herself.

'I know I'll fight lots of things beside rock,' she said. 'I'll be fighting prejudice because of my sex, but I'll get round it somehow — for two reasons. One because I'm dad's daughter and because I want his dream of a Labrador-Land's End Bore to come true; and two, because I believe in this thing we're doing. As far as I am concerned the worst is over. There can't be any blow as violent as losing father . . . ' She paused, then added, 'Unless I lost you as well. If that happened I don't think I could carry on.'

Exmoor went over to her and his arm went about her shoulders. He turned her to face him, looking into her serious face. Then he kissed her gently.

'Of many things you've said, Judy, that's the nicest. Right now, before you get involved officially as Engineer-in-Charge, Canada, we ought to go out and sample normal life for a bit.'

'I can't! Look at the desk — the work I've got to do — '

'I've got plenty too, but it can wait for a few hours. Besides, I — ' Exmoor hesitated briefly. 'I have some shopping to do, at a jeweller's. The third finger of your left hand looks as though it needs some decoration.'

Judy was silent, looking at him.

'There's no reason why we shouldn't become engaged,' Exmoor said stubbornly. 'Maybe it's soon after your dad's death, but on the other hand you'll do better with the thought of a man in your life on whom you can call if need be — even if he is three thousand miles away. I'm sure your dad would want it. We both have to take what opportunities we can on a job like this.'

Judith turned and picked up her things; then suddenly remembering she switched on the intercom.

'Miss Selby? I have to go out for a couple of hours. Take a note of anything important.'

'Yes, Miss Saunders.'

★ ★ ★

Exmoor left Judith at nightfall and flew back on the strato-express to England. His mind was dominated by one thought — he and Judith were engaged. Some time before the Bore was completed they would be married; it all depended on when they both felt they could take time off from the responsibilities they were shouldering. That time was not yet: anything but.

Reflecting on the matter between times, Exmoor was conscious of a vague surprise. Originally, when he had first seen Judith, he had made up his mind to marry her. Yet she had done all the talking, made all the moves, and generally acted in a manner usually left to the man. Not that it made any difference in the long run, but somehow Exmoor felt as though he had been cheated out of something. Upon reflection he could only come to the conclusion that Judith was very like her father in some things. If she felt she wanted a thing, she got it — no matter what.

Something of this side of her nature was evident in the days that followed. Though Exmoor was not personally connected with her Canadian activities, he read enough in the papers of the girl's lone stand against the Bore Corporation when it came to the point of electing a new Canadian engineer to take charge. Though, basically, it was obvious that Judith knew the most, there were nevertheless three skilled engineers who were put forward as successors to Henry Saunders.

In boardroom and at the conference table, Judith orally fought the lot of them. She put up convincing arguments, she displayed her undoubted engineering ability, and her trump card was her knowledge of what her father had planned to do had he lived. In the end she won, mainly because Douglas Lovelace himself — who had always had a sneaking admiration for her — swung the Corporation members into his own line of thinking . . . So a month after her father's death Judith was in his place, officially and absolutely in charge of the Canadian end.

Exmoor televised his congratulations — and his love — and went to work with a new heart. The only difference from now on would be that instead of having a rival — as he had had in Henry Saunders — he would have a girl who needed him, who would not for a moment countenance a desperate race in order to get the Bore finished. The job would be done without any gambles — steadily, efficiently.

100 miles forward — 3,000 feet down. That was the position the following August; and at the Canadian end the progress was about the same. So far as

Canada was concerned, everything was going well; but on the British side something unexpected had cropped up, and the first signs of it appeared as the advance drill-men continued their usual day-by-day battle against the everlasting rock.

Lacy, in charge, was in the midst of directing operations as usual when he became aware of something different. For one thing the drills no longer shrieked as they drove forward. It was as though they were driving into thick mud — something that had none of the adamancy of granite and gneiss.

The men operating the drills shouted soundlessly at each other and pointed forward in the searchlights' glare. Lacy swung round from his position and stared ahead. Either the drills were driving through into space, or else they had come up against something remarkably malleable. Even as he thought of these possibilities he gave the signal for the drills to be stopped.

Silence — or rather a comparative silence. The conveyor belts still rattled;

trucks came back and forth; mechanical navvies shovelled gargantuan mouthfuls of disintegrated rock . . .

Lacy went forward and stared at the rock face with the motionless drills withdrawn from it. The drill-men came stumbling over to him and gazed also, all of them unable to credit what they saw. And yet it was there — a soft yellow wall, glinting where the drills had cleaved so easily through it.

'By all the saints!' one of the drill men gasped at last. 'Look at it! That isn't rock — it's gold!'

'A wall of gold!' another man exclaimed. 'Hey, men — !'

'Shut up!' Lacy commanded, turning. 'Keep your tongue to yourself. We don't want a riot down here.'

The drill man stared stupidly. 'Riot? Why should there be?'

'Obvious, isn't it?' Lacy snapped. 'Let these half-baked workers know that there's wealth here for the picking up and they'll go berserk! No more Bore, no more of this stinking heat, no more danger . . . No, we've got to keep this quiet. Let's see how far it extends.'

Probes were made — careful probes that lasted nearly a couple of hours. The results were astonishing. The wall was nine feet thick, one hundred feet high, and a mile in width. All of it solid gold. Lacy looked rather shaken when at last these findings were reported.

'Okay,' he said quietly. 'I can't keep this sort of thing under my hat! I've got to report it to Mr. Exmoor. This gold is Corporation property. And remember, not a word to anybody!'

Lacy strode off actively, the lights reflecting from his steel helmet. The men who had done the probing watched him go — and so did several others. By this time the very quietness of the non-active drills had attracted attention. It didn't require genius to realize that some thing was different. Amongst themselves the workers began to ask questions. Conveyor men, excavator men — and finally transport men. Particularly Arthur Lovelace. The stoppage of work more than interested him as he delivered a load of Steel-X struts to the rock face.

'What's wrong?' he asked one of the waiting drill men.

'Nothing much.' The man gave a shrug. 'Just waiting for a new plan. We're not boring straight.'

Arthur Lovelace glanced about him, then at the rock face. He gave a start.

'Funniest looking yellow rock I ever saw,' he commented, going closer. 'It looks just like — '

'On your way, Lovelace,' the delivery manager interrupted. 'Get the next load here as quick as you can.'

Lovelace did not move. Instead he grinned and glanced again at the rock face.

'Okay, don't hurry me. I'll move when I'm good and ready.'

'You'll move when I tell you, and that's now!' the delivery manager snapped. 'On your way!'

'This stuff's gold, isn't it?' Lovelace asked casually; and at that the delivery manager — who knew the facts — looked at the other assembled men.

'Yellow metal of some sort; it's got to be checked,' one of the drill men said.

'Better do as you're told, Lovelace, and get going.'

Instead Lovelace looked back at the various workers, all busy with their various tasks. He let out a sudden yell, clearly heard in the comparative quietness.

'Gold, for the picking up, boys! What are you waiting for?'

The men glanced up in surprise. The delivery manager gripped Lovelace's arm fiercely.

'I told you to get out of here, Lovelace! Are you going to do as you're — '

Lovelace wrenched himself free. 'Shut up, can't you? If you think you're going to scare me away from a gold seam like this you're crazy! Come on, lads, bring your picks and shovels! There's enough gold for all of us!'

Convinced at last that Lovelace meant what he said the hundreds of workers began to move forward, and the moment they saw the gleaming yellow of the wall they knew what it implied. One shouted to the other, Lovelace shouting louder than anybody, and in less than ten minutes a mob of men was hacking and tearing at the yellow metal with every tool on which they could lay hands. In less than ten minutes a hundred men were at work, constantly being augmented by others from more distant regions.

Helpless against the horde, the drill men, delivery manager, and the others who had given their word to remain silent about the gold, stood on one side watching the mad rush as incalculable wealth was torn out of the rocks. In the midst of the confusion Lovelace was at work, still shouting, loading gold into his truck as fast as his hands could work . . . until suddenly something prodded him in the back.

'Okay, Lovelace, take it easy!'

Lovelace froze in mid-action. Two lumps of rough gold dropped from his big hands and he straightened up and turned, to find the grim eyes of one of the personnel police upon him. The surrounding men quieted for a moment.

'You're under arrest, Lovelace,' the detective said curtly; then he glanced at two of his armed comrades. 'Escort him to the surface, boys!'

Lovelace whipped his arms free, his unsmiling face a bitter mask.

'Now wait a minute! I've got some say in this — all of us have. We dig this damned tunnel at the orders of those higher up, and the moment we find something valuable we're cheated out of our share! That's what it amounts to!'

'You're right!' one of the workers shouted.

'Dig what you can and get out!' another cried. 'If we don't take the gold the bosses will — !'

'What are we waiting for?'

The personnel detectives hesitated, uncertain of the mood of the men around them — and it was a hesitation that was fatal. Gold is not something from which you can easily shake determined, work-weary men. In consequence the personnel detectives found themselves overwhelmed in a matter of seconds as the angry workers charged them.

It was upon this scene of disorder and struggle that Exmoor and Lacy arrived from the surface. They stopped a few yards from it, staring in amazement.

'What the devil's happened?' Lacy demanded blankly.

'Pretty obvious, isn't it?' Exmoor retorted. 'Somebody's let it be known about the gold — and talking's going to do no good in a case like this.'

Exmoor surveyed for a moment or two more, then he turned and hurried away to the high-perched Protection Squad offices. The staff within, who had been watching the fracas below, turned as he entered.

'Close the section,' Exmoor ordered curtly. 'Fast as you can!'

His orders were instantly obeyed. At the movement of a switch a great wall of Steel-X lowered into place and sealed off the immediate area of the site. Primarily intended for use in case of flooding, or some similar catastrophe, it served just as well as a barrier to human beings.

The dishevelled mob below heard the rumble of the wall as it slid into position and a few were quick enough to dart through the closing gap — but the vast majority were trapped, staring bemusedly around them.

Exmoor studied the crowd for a

moment, then he snatched a mike to him and livened it in contact with big outside speakers.

'Boyd Exmoor speaking,' he said, his voice booming in the cavernous depths. 'I'm out to knock some sense into you — and if I don't get it there'll be gas bombs next and you'll pass out cold. When you awake on the surface you'll have jobs no longer and I'll see to it that your names are blacklisted in every Labour Exchange in the country. I will not tolerate the least relaxation of discipline as long as I'm head of the British section of the Bore project.'

Most of the men were silent, staring upwards. The only one who was not silent was Arthur Lovelace. Exmoor recognized him from his lofty elevation through the open office window.

'Why don't you admit the truth, boss?' Lovelace shouted. 'You're trying with the rest of the high-ups — my father included — to cash in on a gold strike, which would never have been found but for us!'

'You're under arrest, Lovelace,' Exmoor retorted — then he stood watching as the three personnel detectives, free now of the mob, came forward and took Lovelace's arms firmly.

'We arrested him earlier, Mr. Exmoor,' one of the men called up. 'He got the rest of the men behind him and overwhelmed us.'

'When the way's free take him to my office,' Exmoor said; then he continued grimly, 'You're too free with your opinions, Lovelace, both in this instance and others.'

'You can't deny that that barrier is made of gold!' Lovelace shouted.

'I wouldn't attempt to — but to prevent any such disorder as this again I'll tell you something. Over on the Canadian side there was a recent strike of diamonds — but the Corporation decided that a percentage should be given to the workers as well as to the Corporation itself. That will apply in this case. The gold will be taken to the surface, assessed, and a percentage paid to you, the highest amounts going to the drill men as the actual discoverers. So it will be with everything of value we happen on during the journey. That's a new regulation of the Corporation, which I happen to know . . . Any questions?'

'Why weren't we told of this before?' Lovelace demanded.

'There was no need until we hit up against something. Now you know, all of you. Are you going to behave yourselves henceforth?'

There was silence for a moment, then somebody at the back gave a cheer. It was only a matter of moments before most of the men were echoing it.

'Open the section,' Exmoor said; then as the barrier slid back and the men moved back from the gold face he stood watching Lovelace, firm in the grip of the detectives, being led back along the tunnel prior to being removed to the surface.

'He's a born troublemaker, that Lovelace,' one of the Protection men said, shaking his head.

Exmoor did not answer. He left the offices and returned to the ground. When he reached Lacy he found him scratching his head.

'You quieted things down all right,

boss, but that's the first I've ever heard about that new law of the Corporation's.'

'And I,' Exmoor said, with a faint grin. 'I'll have to put it to D.L. as a proposition — the only one possible if we're to keep the workers happy. If we didn't have Arthur Lovelace stirring up trouble we'd have somebody else. Might as well start a share-and-share-alike basis and so cut out troublemakers.'

'Right enough, sir . . . Well, what are my orders regarding this gold?'

'Have it removed, every bit of it, and taken to the surface. Carry on as usual. I'll have a squad of detectives down here to watch over the proceedings, and before any worker returns to the surface he must pass a search test in case he's got gold on him.'

Lacy nodded promptly and strode away towards the waiting drill men. Exmoor surveyed a moment longer, then he ascended to the surface once more — and his office. Within it, sullen and hardmouthed, Arthur Lovelace was waiting, securely held by two of the detectives.

'All right,' Exmoor said briefly, tossing

down his steel helmet. 'Let him go.'

The detectives took their departure. Exmoor moved forward and faced Lovelace directly. The young man returned a brazen stare for a moment then lowered his eyes and searched the boarded floor.

'What in hell's the matter with you, Lovelace?' Exmoor asked at last. 'This is the third time you've caused trouble, and I'm about at the end of my patience.'

'Third time?' Lovelace raised his head. 'How do you make that out? Only trouble I've been in before was when I warned the men about going too fast.'

'Then you've forgotten the little incident when a backfire from your truck ignited fire-damp gas and caused two hundred and seventy men to die?'

It was a long shot but Exmoor considered it worth taking. The expression on Lovelace's face justified him.

'I don't pretend to know what you have against the Bore — or your father,' Exmoor continued, 'but I do know that I'm not going to struggle with you any longer: I've better things to do. The matter is up to your father from now on.'

Lovelace said nothing. Watching him intently, Exmoor picked up the telephone and switched in the private line. In a moment Douglas Lovelace's voice answered.

'Exmoor here, D.L. I need your help.'

'Okay. What's your trouble?'

'Your son, D.L. He's more than I can handle. He's right here beside me now following a riot down below. We ran into a wall of gold and he wasn't slow to cash in on stirring up the workers to attempted theft.'

'Tell me more,' Lovelace growled — so Exmoor gave all the details. He refrained from mentioning only one thing — the matter of the backfire and the fire-damp. Not because he had any particular love for young Lovelace but because he knew the evidence was too slight to maintain a definite accusation.

'Only one thing to do — fire him,' Lovelace said curtly. 'Strike him off the list of workers and tell him to report to me immediately. I'll get to the bottom of his games.'

'Right,' Exmoor assented. 'Sorry to have to do this, D.L., but you told me to inform you if — '

'Okay; you acted rightly. I'll soon straighten the lad out.'

Exmoor rang off and looked at Arthur Lovelace as he stood in silence nearby.

'You're going to report to your father immediately,' Exmoor said curtly. 'And you're struck off our list of workers from here on. That's all — and think yourself lucky to be let off so lightly.'

'Who does the old boy think he is?' Arthur demanded. 'Report to him! I might be a kid of twelve!'

'I'm not going into that. I've told you what to do — and if you take my advice you'll do it.'

Young Lovelace went, slamming the office door. Exmoor sighed, then picked up the telephone again and contacted Roby, of Personnel Security.

'You probably know I've had trouble with young Lovelace again,' Exmoor said. 'Thanks for having your men around to cool him off a bit. Right now his father's going to deal with him, so that lets you out. However, I'm ringing about another matter. We've struck gold in the tunnel. I want you to have a detail of men down there night and day whilst the gold is removed. Every worker is to have a radiation security test before he leaves for home. Okay?'

'I'll fix it right away, Mr. Exmoor. As far as young Lovelace is concerned I've heard what happened. My men have told me. But there's something else you ought to know.'

'Something else?'

'You told me to investigate young Lovelace to the full. Well, I've done it, and the inquiries have produced some pretty interesting details, particularly as we cooperated with Scotland Yard. It might interest you to know that Arthur Lovelace has been working for a powerful political body in Europe for nearly three years. He made his contacts originally when he went to university.'

Exmoor's face became grim. 'So that's it? What you mean is, he's an agent for an enemy of this country?'

'The country I have in mind is an enemy of the entire British Commonwealth. I was going to send in a detailed report for you to study and act upon.'

'How soon can you send it?'

'Give me a couple of hours and it will be on your desk.'

'Right! I'm going to let D.L. know about it. While he's got young Arthur on the carpet he may as well know every fact.'

Exmoor rang off, his mind filled with all kinds of speculations. The news had come as a shock, and yet when he came to think about it, it wasn't so inconceivable. Young Lovelace was a hothead and not at an age for measured thought on any subject. Ruled by an enemy he would be easy game. In one sweep it explained his strange behaviour and his complete disregard for his own or anybody else's safety . . .

Exmoor spent the intervening two hours checking up on the work in the Bore, making sure the gold was being removed and that Roby's squad of men had arrived to supervise the proceedings. All seemed to be well in that direction — but before very long the men would be asking about their cut in the gold find. That was yet another thing that had to be fixed.

119

Under the two hours, Roby's report was sent. Exmoor read it through, and he saw enough to convince him that an interview with Lovelace personally was called for. So he left the site of operations to take care of itself and headed in his fast car to London.

He found Douglas Lovelace as business-like as usual, but obviously somewhat troubled by the unsavoury business of his son.

'What's on your mind, Boyd?' he asked, shaking hands. 'We've only just phoned each other.'

'I know that, D.L., but I've got some information here that I wouldn't trust to the 'phone, not even the private line. It's about Arthur.'

Lovelace grimaced. 'What — again! I've only just finished dealing with him. I've fired him completely — told him he's never to go anywhere near the Bore again. Dammit, the boy behaves like a lunatic. He's rank poison to a project like ours.'

'You've turned him loose in the city, then?' Exmoor asked grimly, as he snapped the clamps on his brief case and took out the Roby report. 'You'd better make moves to have him picked up as soon as possible. As long as he's roaming free he's a menace. Here — read this!'

With vague astonishment on his face Lovelace took the report. The astonishment passed to grimness, and by the time he had finished the steel-trap mouth was clamped shut.

'We might as well face it,' Exmoor said bluntly. 'Your son is a paid agent — a professional saboteur. You can see from the report just how far things have gone. The Bore has got to be smashed at all costs, and — though there may be others at work — your son is the chief wrecker.'

'But it's incredible! That my own son could be doing this!'

'Incredible it may be, but the Personnel department and Scotland Yard don't make mistakes. There it is before you. Arthur has tried to break up the Bore project since its inception. He's so blindly devoted to our enemies that he'll even commit suicide in the belief he's serving the Cause.'

Lovelace got to his feet and strode

angrily about the office.

'Let me get this in focus. These enemies of ours — a whole flock of European countries — don't want the Bore to succeed because in the event of war we'll have a nuclear-proof lifeline direct to Europe, down which we can transport men, machines, and provisions. They are employing agents in both Britain and Canada to do all they can to foment strikes and unrest, and if possible wreck the entire project. On the English side my son is a leading light because of his close connection to me and consequent immunity from suspicion.'

'That's it,' Exmoor agreed, his eyes hard. 'Up to now, your son has done three things — first, he tried to begin a go-slow policy, which I broke up; second, he was responsible for the death of 270 men in the fire-damp explosion; and third, he tried to begin a riot, which would soon have spread, over this wall of gold business.'

'Killed 270 men? What the devil do you mean?'

Exmoor gave the facts and concluded:

'I have no evidence, but the facts fit just the same. Son or no son, D.L., you've got to have Arthur picked up and put in a safe place. If you don't he'll cause more trouble.'

'Not now he won't. He's finished with the Bore: I told you that. He'll not be permitted within miles of it.'

Exmoor gave a grim smile. 'What do you imagine he's going to do now you're through with him?'

'I've no idea. He'll find work somehow in the city — either in his University capacity, or else as a truck driver.'

'I'll lay a bet,' Exmoor said, flattening his palm on the desk. 'I'll gamble that Arthur will fly straight to Europe, tell his masters of the mess he's in, and get fresh instructions. There's nothing to stop him — no police prevention, nothing. He's obsessed with political poison and he's got to destroy the Bore. That's the only thing he lives for. The fact that he's been thrown out of the Bore will only make him the more determined.'

The industrialist was silent for a moment, wrestling with the unpalatable fact that his son was an enemy and completely in the grip of the powers controlling him.

'Let him go free and you'll have no Bore,' Exmoor snapped. 'That will be the end of it.'

Abruptly, Lovelace seemed to decide. He picked up the 'phone.

'Get me Scotland Yard — international Division . . . ' He waited, his eyes looking into distance; then he continued, 'Douglas Lovelace here. I want you to pick up my son immediately, wherever he may be in London. Arrest him on a charge of spying. When you get him I'll supply the details . . . '

Mechanically Lovelace put the telephone down again and then gave himself a little shake.

'They'll do it?' Exmoor ventured.

'Yes, they'll do it. My name's well known enough to ensure immediate action.'

Exmoor nodded slowly, then he gripped Lovelace's arm. 'I'm sorry, D.L. I know exactly how you must be feeling.'

The industrialist sat down again and forced himself to awareness of the moment.

'Anything else whilst you're here, Boyd, or would you consider that enough?'

'More than enough — but there is one more thing. We can save a lot of trouble amongst the men if we share out on everything of value we find during the boring. You agreed, with the Canadian end, on a share out on that recent strike of carbon and tungsten. I think the same thing should be done for the gold we've now found. A percentage to the Corporation and the remainder to the workers, increasing the amount in respect of those who made the original find.'

Lovelace sighed. 'All right, if you think it's advisable.'

'Definitely I do. It's only by keeping the workers contented that we'll get results — and they won't be so inclined to subversive talk if they think they're being well looked after.'

'Right . . . ' Lovelace looked moodily in front of him. 'I'll see that it's made into a legal order.'

'Then that's all, D.L. I'll be on my way.'

'Fair enough . . . ' Then Lovelace

added surprisingly, 'I wonder what the Bore will take from us next, Boyd? It has the qualities of a Frankenstein monster, don't you think?'

'I don't quite follow you, sir.'

'I mean that it seems to take everything of value away. It took Henry Saunders, for one thing — one of the world's best engineers. It's taken the lives of two hundred and seventy workers and ruined their families. It has an ever increasing demand for more labour — and more — and more! Regardless of race or creed. The Bore's never satisfied. It consumes an astronomical amount of money and as yet we're only one hundred miles forward . . . Now it's taken my son. I wonder what it will demand next?'

Exmoor did not answer. He felt uncomfortable.

'All right, forget it,' Lovelace sighed. 'Get on with the job, Boyd. If you need me I'll be ready.'

Exmoor went, in a curiously sober frame of mind.

5

Unexpected barrier

By October the Bore had progressed
500 miles forward; and by the end of
November 600 miles had been covered
and a depth of 8,000 feet penetrated.
True, it had been comparatively easy.
Rock all the time with no dangerous
seams. From three original Astley drills
the number had now increased to sixteen,
working day and night. Men had fallen
out and been replaced. Always the labour
numbers were kept up, and provision
made for those unfortunates who had
succumbed to permanent injury as a
consequence of their work in the Bore
. . . Money was swallowed up in staggering amounts, making the original budget
seem ridiculous, but the fact remained
that everybody — well or unwell — had
to be cared for. The Bore was a matter for
world concern now, and though they did

not like it the trust corporations, the bankers, and the tycoons had to hand out. Eventually — eventually — they would collect huge dividends, and this was the glittering prize that attracted them.

The weeks had been filled to the limit with work for Boyd Exmoor. He was here, there, and everywhere, arranging this, deciding the other, constantly in contact with the G-men (geologists) as they probed the way ahead. Only occasionally did he find time to talk to and see Judith Saunders, to find that she too was in the thick of it — perhaps even more so for she was constantly fighting a silent battle against prejudice as well. More than one newspaper and television channel had made it clear that her sex was against her in such a tremendous task — to be immediately contradicted by those who supported her. Plainly, subversive elements were at work trying to get rid of her, but so far without effect. She worked on, and under her direction Canada moved onwards again, not far behind the British total.

That the strain of work had affected Judith was obvious to Exmoor, even through the cold medium of television. She was no longer the smiling, brightly intelligent girl she had been. She was a mature woman worn with responsibilities, her eyes critical and her speech sharp. Only on very rare occasions did she mention the engagement that she and Exmoor had wished on themselves, even though she still wore the ring that Exmoor had bought her. Matters connected with her personal life seemed to be on another plane entirely.

It worried Exmoor, but there was nothing he could do about it.

Matters were too pressing at the British end these days to permit of any more flying visits to Canada to check up on romance.

And Arthur Lovelace? He seemed to have vanished utterly. A search for him was in progress day and night, but by this time Scotland Yard was reasonably satisfied that he had left the country before they had been advised to get on his track. Lovelace senior accepted the position. At least his son was now nowhere near the Bore and that was the main thing . . .

At the same time, in various directions, the personnel men were investigating every man who seemed to be causing more than his share of trouble. He might have been an enemy agent; he might not.

Taking no chances, such men were removed and barred from future service on the Bore. Britain and Canada both adopted the same tactics.

December 1st. Down 8,250 feet. In twenty-four more days it would be Christmas up above, away from this madness of suffocating heat and maddening noise. The time when, all being well, the workers would want a few hours off with their families, where the life of a human mole could be forgotten —

Exmoor started as the telephone jangled at his elbow. He had just been reflecting on approaching Christmas, and the fact that by now his end of the Bore was more than halfway to the central rendezvous . . . And the estimate had been for ten years!

'Hello?' He held the telephone and

waited. Lacy's voice came through, heavy with controlled fury.

'You'd better come, sir. Trouble, I'm afraid. The drills are chewed up.'

'Chewed!' Exmoor exclaimed. 'But that isn't possible! Not with Steel-X.'

'Fact remains it's happened, sir.'

Exmoor did not waste any more time on the telephone. He grabbed his helmet and left the office. Within ten minutes — since by now his office occupied a near position in the shaft — he was at the rock face. He glanced at the idling men hanging around their huge drills and then he went over to Lacy, to find him in the midst of examining one of the drills. It looked like so much pulped metal, somehow crushed inwards from some terrific force.

'There it is, sir.' Lacy gave a bitter glance. 'And every one of the drills is alike.'

Exmoor examined the mangled remains and then gave an incredulous glance. 'How could this happen, man? Steel-X is proof against anything. What are you boring through?'

'The G-boys said it was another lot of granite. We started the drills up this morning and in a matter of ten minutes this was what happened. All sixteen of them broke at about the same time.'

Exmoor looked at the silent monsters looming away into the searchlighted distance. They alone were silent: the rest of the vast industry was going on as usual.

'This would never happen on granite,' Exmoor said. 'Better see what Mart Astley has to say. Where is he?'

'I took the liberty of sending out a call for him, sir. He was with the G-men last I heard of him — Ah, here he is now.'

The gaunt figure of the metallurgist came into view. As usual he looked tired. He asked no questions to begin with, but picked the broken drill from the portable table. Presently he looked up, his eyes asking a dozen questions.

'Pretty, isn't it?' Lacy snapped. 'Damned sabotage if you ask me!'

'Why do you say that?' Astley inquired.

'It's the only possible answer. These drills of yours will go through anything on earth. Somehow, during the night shift when I was off duty, the drills must have been switched.'

'Switched?' Exmoor repeated.

'Yes. The real drills somehow smuggled away and fresh ones, of normal steel, put in their place. Naturally, they won't take it.'

'So that's what you think, is it? That there's been dirty work on all sixteen drills during the night shift?' Exmoor shook his head. 'I can't believe that, Lacy: it'd be too difficult a job.'

'It wouldn't if overseer and men were working in conjunction. I wouldn't trust a damned soul down here these days!'

'Not all the men, perhaps, but Burgess I'd trust with my life,' Exmoor said. 'Don't let things run away with you, Lacy. I know you've good reason to be jumpy after some of the things that have happened, but — '

'There's got to be another answer.' Martin Astley said, looking at the smashed drill again with a lens screwed in his eye.

Nobody spoke for a moment. The idea of sabotage was gravely disturbing, and it was an idea which Exmoor did not want to credit because it could involve so many people — Then Astley spoke again, his voice a mixture of amazement and relief.

'It isn't sabotage, Lacy, so you can forget it. This drill is Steel-X: I know it well enough to recognize it through this lens.'

He took the lens out of his eye and stood thinking. Lacy gave him an astounded look.

'But your drills will go through granite as easily as cheese, sir. Why should they buckle?'

Astley shrugged. 'Only one answer — they must have struck something that is a thousand times harder than granite!'

Lacy gave a bewildered glance towards the rock face. There were sixteen holes in it — big, ragged holes created by the drills first, boring in, and then being withdrawn in a broken condition. Exmoor and Astley looked at the rock face too, and for Exmoor the mystery was as complete as it was for Lacy.

Then Astley acted. He picked up a powerful torch from the table, went over to the rock face, and shone the beam through one of the ragged holes. After perhaps four feet the beam struck the darkness of the unbored rock — or so it seemed. In each drilled hole the answer was the same. Approximately four feet of depth and then blackness, and it was that blackness which was tough enough to chew Steel-X as though it were malleable lead.

'Well?' Exmoor asked at last, becoming impatient with the delay. 'What's the next move, Mart?'

'Have your men clear away this granite. They'll have to do manually since drills might pierce beyond it and get smashed up again. We've got to clear the granite before we can find out what's behind it and analyze it.'

'Makes you wonder what the hell good geologists are,' Lacy grunted, looking at Exmoor. 'They said granite ahead and we run into a mess like this!'

'I don't think you can blame the G-men,' Astley said, as unmoved as ever. 'They didn't anticipate anything like this lying behind the actual granite seam.' He looked at Exmoor. 'Up to you, Boyd. I can't do anything until your men clear the way.'

'Okay,' Exmoor said, with a glance at Lacy. 'Get them started.'

The foreman did not waste any time — and neither did the men with him to direct them. Every available man and tool was pressed into service and the granite face was attacked with untiring energy. The job was obviously going to be a long one, so Exmoor returned to his executive office, only coming back to the site in the late afternoon when a call from Astley advised him that the job was done — sufficiently anyhow to get a clearance to the mysterious black barrier.

Arriving back at the site, Exmoor gazed at the substance now revealed. It was greyish black, rather like indifferent coal. Astley, who had already made preliminary tests of the stuff with a variety of complicated instruments, gave Exmoor a wry look as he turned.

'Got you foxed, Boyd?' he asked. 'You don't know what it is?'

'Hanged if I do!' Exmoor scraped at it

experimentally with a small chisel. 'It's certainly mighty hard!'

'There's no blame attaches to you because you don't recognize it,' Astley said. 'These G-boys don't know what it is, either . . . ' He glanced at them standing rather shame-faced in a semicircle. 'The stuff is neutronium, and the only place you're likely to find it — excluding the depths of space or within the interior of a white dwarf star — is right here, eight thousand feet down and under tremendous pressure.'

'Neutronium?' Exmoor repeated, frown-ing. 'I seem to have heard of it, but it's only a theoretical substance, isn't it? Some-thing composed entirely of neutrons with the normal electrons stripped off because of overwhelming pressure?'

'Pressure or furious heat both produce the same effect,' the metallurgist said. 'It's an inconceivably dense metal, so dense that a cubic inch of it would weigh about one ton.'

'What!' Exmoor exclaimed, staring — and Astley gave his tired smile.

'I thought that would shake you. This metal — if you can call it that — is actually pure matter, earth substance. There are bare nuclei in its composition, and hardly any electrons — as there usually are. This compression produces vast weight in comparison to size. You'll find a similar substance in space — the Companion of Sirius to be exact. However, it can happen inside a planet due to the surrounding pressure.'

Exmoor said blankly, 'No wonder Steel-X buckled!'

'Yes — no wonder! How far this neutronium barrier extends we don't know, but if we're to have any tunnel at all we've got to shift it.'

'With every cubic inch weighing a ton!' exclaimed Lacy, who had been listening in wonder. 'It just can't be done!'

'It can be, and it will be,' Astley replied patiently. 'I'm the scientist of this project and it's up to me to devise ways and means. But I'll tell you one thing, Boyd — ' He looked at Exmoor seriously. 'It's going to mean a considerable delay whilst we figure out the necessary machinery. A lot of men will have to be laid off — the drill men for instance.'

'What machinery are you thinking of?' Exmoor asked.

'Electrical. No ordinary machines can do anything with neutronium. Even if we could isolate it from the surrounding granite we'd never be able to cut it, blast it, or lift it. The only way out is to convert it into normal matter — supply it with the electrons with which it is deficient.'

Exmoor did not grasp the point, and his face must have showed it for Astley continued,

'Leave it to me, Boyd. It's a job for a physicist, which qualifications I have. It's simply a problem in nuclear physics. I have to devise a machine for adding electrons to this mass. By that means it will become ordinary matter and can then be removed — but how long it's going to take me I don't know. So make arrangements for an indefinite delay.'

And with that Exmoor had to be satisfied. He could not thrash the matter out with Astley because his knowledge was insufficient — so he fell back on ordering away redundant men to the surface until the time came for recall.

Then began Astley's long scientific investigation into the problem, helped by teams of physicists called in specially to consider the problem.

Christmas — that festive period on which Exmoor had banked for a brief jollification on the part of all Bore workers — came and went under a sombre cloud. Martin Astley and his team ignored the season and went on working out details . . . But in other directions there was an air of sombre quietness. More men ceased work each day as progress remained halted. There even crept into the newspapers a hint that the British end of the Bore was closed for good — that the engineers had hit up against some invincible barrier but were not immediately admitting the fact.

Exmoor considered he did the right thing in refuting this belief, both in newspapers and television. He calmed too the deeply worried Douglas Lovelace, up to his neck in financial commitments — and that automatically brought relief to the various other monetary trusts and syndicates who were involved.

On the other side of the picture the enemies of the Bore were at work — the hundred and one little men and women who were in the employ of unfriendly nations and who did their level best to stir up unrest out of the impasse that had been reached. There was no actual demonstration, no actual violence, but there was that growing undercurrent of discontent as week followed week, into the New Year, and men drifted about the surface, workless, and with only a thin subsistence allowance to maintain them and their families until work should begin again.

Exmoor talked to them personally: he staged special television meetings. He did everything one strong man could do to hold things together — and whenever he could he coaxed, urged, and even bullied Martin Astley and his team of physicists. Anything to hurry them up. He might as well have tried to shift the sun. Astley went on working calmly, sorting out details, spending endless hours in concentrated thought . . .

In mid-January, knowing that his

absence would not be felt in the present conditions, Exmoor gave himself a brief holiday — and naturally he went to Canada. There he made the galling discovery — though he did not permit it to show in his expression — that the Canadians were making almost fantastic progress in their drive to the central rendezvous. They were about 10,000 feet down and boring without interruption, the whole vast enterprise a seething anthill of prodigious activity.

Calm and resourceful at the head of it all was Judith Saunders — but somehow she was not the Judith Saunders she had been. In some odd way she seemed commercialized, become a part of the project he was directing, and much of the criticism she had been compelled to fight had hardened her nature. Looking at her in her executive office Exmoor realized with a shock that he had not been mistaken in his assessment of her from his television screen. It had not been just the mechanical intermediary: she definitely was different in an inexplicable way.

'How long, Boyd,' she asked, relaxing

behind her desk, 'do you think this English hold-up is going to last, anyway? It's nearly six weeks now, isn't it.'

'Yes.' Exmoor shook his head and sighed. 'I've no idea. You know the kind of man Mart Astley is: he wouldn't hurry even if he were seated on an H-bomb about to explode. I've just got to possess myself in patience, as everybody else has.'

'As you've seen, we're all right.' There was obvious pride in the girl's tone. 'Our progress has been rapid, and if our geologists are to be believed there's nothing very tough ahead of us . . . ' She stopped and gave a direct look. 'If we reach the central rendezvous first we're not going any further. Our contract doesn't call for it. We'll wait until you meet us.'

'We'll be there,' Exmoor said quietly, 'even if we are delayed as at present.'

Silence for a moment. They both sat looking at each other. Then Exmoor said, 'Ten years sounds rather a silly estimate now, don't you think? The job will be done in two, I think.'

'Perhaps. I'm a cautious soul, as you

know. I'm not fool enough to think that because we've had unbroken progress so far we'll have it all the time. Look what happened to you! It can happen to us.'

Exmoor got to his feet, hesitated a fraction, then went round the desk and caught the girl by the shoulders. Her grey eyes looked up in brief surprise — then she relaxed a little and put up a hand to Exmoor's as he grasped her.

'Thanks, Boyd,' she said simply. 'I'd begun to think we'd both forgotten.'

'Forgotten?'

'Forgotten that once we behaved as though romance meant something — even to the extent of your buying this.' Judith held forth her hand with the engagement ring upon it. 'This Bore seems to have changed things somehow — all in a few months.'

'It hasn't changed things for me and it never will. I feel precisely the same about you as I ever did: my only regret is that we can't see more of each other.'

'That's what I mean — the Bore is between us, and will remain so until it's finished. After that . . . Well, you don't suppose that will be the end, do you?'

Puzzled, Exmoor took his arm from Judith's shoulders and sat down close beside her. Her face was pale, unsmiling. There were even streaks of grey in the dark hair above her ears. She looked like a woman who has been driving herself endlessly.

'It'll be the end when we've finished the Bore, Judy.'

'So you think that, do you? You haven't thought ahead, as I have. The end will be the beginning. You don't suppose big business is going to say 'Thanks very much' and let it go at that when the Bore's finished, do you? No, Boyd. We're both too valuable. We'll be raked in to direct the building of the track for the Cannon Ball Express. We'll be consulted about pedestrian ways and traffic avenues. It'll go on and on, then suddenly one day we'll realize that we're still working and that we're old. Too old.'

Exmoor was silent, secretly amazed at the sombreness — and accuracy — of her speculations.

'When you deliver yourself to the Bore,

it takes everything,' Judith sighed. 'I never realized it so clearly since I took over father's mantle. It's like that sign on prisons — 'Abandon hope, all ye who enter here'.'

Exmoor stirred restlessly. He was haunted by a memory of what Douglas Lovelace had said — 'The Bore has something of the qualities of Frankenstein's monster, don't you think? I wonder what it will take from us next?'

'You're tired, Judy,' Exmoor said at last, falling back on the obvious. 'You're just taking a defeatist view because it's the easiest. You feel the strain more as a woman . . . I tell you this: the Bore ceases to be a part of our lives once it is through. There are other engineers who can tackle the remainder.'

'I hope you're right,' Judith said, looking into the distance. 'For myself, I don't think I'll ever be able to detach myself.'

'I'll see that you do! When the Bore's complete we're going to get married and then take a long rest. I'll do all the detaching necessary.'

'You haven't got your father's dream always before you,' Judith said, with a faint smile. 'I have. That's the difference.'

'What difference?'

'Just building his half of the tunnel was only the beginning for dad. He planned out the railway tracks, the pedestrian ways, the traffic levels, the rest centres — everything to the smallest detail. I feel I shall be failing him if I don't complete everything as he intended it to be completed.'

Exmoor frowned, 'But hang it all, Judy, he wasn't the kind of man to expect you to sacrifice your life and happiness on an ideal which was primarily his. It's different for a man — he plans his life on achievements. It's not a woman's job. Your loyalty is misplaced, and Henry Saunders would be the first man to say so.'

Judith said nothing. She seemed as though she wanted to say something more, but did not quite know how. At last Exmoor took her hand in his.

'No more of this, Judy,' he said firmly. 'You're mine, and I'm yours — and the

Bore isn't going to stop it. Right?'

She did not answer. Exmoor transferred his hand to her chin and tilted her face upwards gently.

'Right?' he repeated, smiling.

She looked at him for a full fifteen seconds, and manlike it astonished him to see tears slowly filling her eyes. Abruptly her reserve seemed to go and she collapsed on his shoulder, sobbing as heavily as at that moment when she had heard of her father's death.

'Judy dearest, what is it?' Exmoor's big hands stroked her hair tenderly. 'What's wrong?'

'Ev — everything! I'm so weary, Boyd — so sick of everything! I would to heaven I'd never seen the Bore! But for dad I'd stop right now, but I can't as it is . . . I must go on! I've got to!'

Exmoor held her a little away from him so he could study her tear-stained face.

'Now look here, Judy, this won't do. You're going to give yourself a nervous breakdown if you're not careful! Why, your nerves are in rags. You've got to rest; put in a deputy. See a doctor and have

148

him make it compulsory.'

'There's nobody who can do things the way I'd do them, Boyd. Don't you understand? I've got to — ' Judith swung impatiently as the telephone rang. Handkerchief dabbing at her eyes she answered as quietly as she could. 'Yes — Judith Saunders here.'

For a moment or two she listened then listlessly held the instrument out to Exmoor. He took it.

'Exmoor here.' He listened, his expression changing to one of enthusiasm. 'Right, I'll come back right away. Be with you in a few hours.'

He downed the instrument onto its cradle and looked at the girl. She had recovered herself now but her eyes were still wet.

'Not trouble, I hope?' she asked anxiously; and at that Exmoor laughed and caught her shoulders in his arms for a moment.

'Trouble? Lord, no! The best news in the world! Old Astley has at last come to life with an answer and we're going to start shifting the neutronium barrier the moment I get back to England. I've got to fly . . . ' He withdrew his face from kissing the girl. 'And remember, dearest — rest! Promise?'

'I'll try,' she said quietly. 'I can't say more than that.'

Exmoor sighed. 'For both our sakes I beg of you to slow up. I'll keep watch over you on the televisor and if you don't do as you're told I'll desert everything and come back here and deal with you myself . . . You're more to me than any Bore!'

Judith laughed — briefly like her old self. Then she was lifted protestingly out of her chair as Exmoor's powerful arms closed about her . . .

6

Flood!

It was late evening when at length Exmoor returned to the British site of operations. He found things relatively quiet, save for the army of men at work lining the completed parts with Steel-X. At the rock face — or rather neutronium-face — itself he discovered Martin Astley himself, together with a scattering of engineers and physicists, the men who had worked exclusively on the problem of the barrier.

'Glad you've shown up,' Astley said rather drily, as Exmoor appeared. 'Why you had to go to Canada with so much on hand I'll never know.'

Exmoor shrugged. 'No use in hanging around. Anyway, what have you got to show me?'

'The answer to our troubles, I think. Here are the machines which will supply the electrons to this mass . . . '

Astley waved his hand to three curious-looking pieces of equipment, not unlike drills in design but having lensed fronts instead of revolving drill spindles. From them there snaked back a multitude of wires that in turn linked to a portable switchboard and then to a massive distant generator.

'I'm not going into all the scientific details because they don't matter,' Astley said. 'You want results, not words. I'll sum it up by saying that once these machines are switched on they'll bombard this neutronium barrier here with electrons. Then a transmutation will take place.'

'Actually then,' Exmoor said, 'it's transmutation of elements on a big scale?'

'Uh-huh — you can call it that. The machines can transmute lead into gold if we decided to do it, but that's a fantastic side issue — and a damned dangerous one, too. Our job is to wipe out this neutronium by altering it. We've decided to convert it into lead. Then it will be easy and malleable to remove.'

'Good . . . And you're ready to tackle the job now?'

'It won't take more than fifteen minutes.' A shadow of hesitation passed over Astley's face. 'So far as we can figure there won't be any danger. However, there's always the unknown factor in these things and so I think we'll get to a safe distance and do everything by remote control.'

Exmoor nodded. He was pretty well powerless in this act and had to leave everything to Astley and the men whose job it was. A general retreat up the tunnel took place, Astley carrying with him a small radio-control box. When finally he had selected a high vantage nearly three quarters of a mile from the neutronium wall he nodded and looked back at the searchlighted barrier.

'This ought to do. We can still see the barrier but we're clear of any trouble it might cause.'

'What about emanations?' Exmoor asked. 'Is there going to be any excess of radioactivity?'

'Most unlikely. This is not an explosion, Boyd — it's an implosion. We're adding — not disintegrating.' Astley steadied himself, the physicists watching intently around him. 'Here we go — and keep your fingers crossed.'

With that Astley depressed the buttons on the radio-control box he was carrying. Exmoor gazed in silent interest as, in the distance, switches and controls moved and shifted on the portable switchboard. In response the 'transmutation machines' themselves swung into position and glowing colour bulbs leapt into life to announce that the machine was 'live'.

More movements on his radio-control box, then Astley gave a satisfied sigh as a thin, high whining note came from the three machines themselves. There was nothing visible, only that distracting edgy sound increasing in intensity with every second.

'Hold your ears!' Astley said briefly, as Exmoor winced. 'This is going to get a lot worse yet — We're more or less attuned to it.'

Exmoor felt in his pocket for the earplugs he always carried. Once they were in place the din lessened. He watched Astley and the physicists and engineers hastily plug their own ears and then resume watching. Still the din increased, and then the neutronium barrier itself gradually began to change visibly. Threads of purple colour veined their way through the greyness; then came curious splotches of crimson, which pulsated like mysterious hearts. Astley watched this phenomenon for a while and then shouted something. Due to the earplugs he was inaudible, but evidently something urgent was on his mind for he switched off the radio box abruptly —

Then came disaster! In a sudden flash, so quick the eye could not follow it, the colour traceries in the neutronium became one and spread to the whole mass. At the same moment the mass moved sideways and upwards simultaneously, like some monstrous coloured balloon inflated at ultra-rapid speed.

So much Exmoor had time to notice — time enough in which to feel fear. Then the lot exploded in a blinding torrent of blue light. Rock flew through the air; underpinnings snapped like matches. In a hail of destruction the roof started to fall inwards.

Exmoor went down beneath a rain of débris, catching a brief glimpse of the physicists and engineers toppling from their various positions. Even as he fell, and yet was unhurt, Exmoor realized that he had dropped in the hollow of two rocks, and a massive boulder had bridged itself over the top of them, saving him from the deluge that crashed inwards. The noise was catastrophic and the darkness bewildering. Exmoor tore the earplugs out of his ears and breathed hard, wondering where he was and whether he was going to get out of this alive.

Dust, lashed by a fierce blast, blew into his face, stinging his skin and setting him coughing — then the disturbance seemed to abate except for a curious rumbling noise like far distant thunder.

He stirred, found he was miraculously unhurt, and reached clawing hands into the darkness. Then he listened. Something was stirring near him, audible above the mysterious distant rumbling.

'Do I hear somebody?' demanded a

voice from the blackness.

'Martin! It's you, isn't it?'

'Yes, it's me,' agreed the laconic voice.

'How are you fixed? Badly hurt?'

'I'm not hurt at all. How about you?'

'My legs seem to be out of action: can't tell if I've got any. Hell, we need a light.'

Exmoor struggled forward again, pushing aside heavy rock in the darkness. He came at last on Astley and felt his arms and body quickly. The rest seemed to be rock.

'Don't — don't waste your time,' the metallurgist said, breathing hard. 'I've got half the tunnel on me from the waist down.'

'You'll be all right,' Exmoor told him. 'I'll get you out.'

With that he felt around the rocks and began to shove them to one side. There seemed to be infinite numbers of them, and though he worked furiously there didn't seem to be any sign of them getting less. Astley's gasping voice came to him at intervals amidst his struggles.

'I'm one prize idiot, Boyd — no other way for it. I should have known! The

157

— the unknown factor I told you about — '

'What unknown factor?' Exmoor questioned, turning towards the pained voice in the blackness.

'The neutronium — as it changed its state it expanded enormously. Naturally it would do: I realize that now. It was compressed because of the absence of electrons. When those became added it tripled — tripled and quadrupled its size. Expanded upwards, downwards, and sideways — God, my back!'

There was silence for a moment, except for anguished, rasping breathing. Exmoor returned to his attack on the rocks, then he stopped again, listening to that noise like distant thunder. It had suddenly increased in volume.

'What do you make of that noise?' he asked, puzzled. 'Is it some hangover from the explosion?'

'It's the ocean, man! Flooding into the shaft!'

'The ocean!'

'No other answer. As the neutronium expanded upwards it must have penetrated the seabed. Now it's — ' Astley stopped suddenly, his breath wheezing. Then abruptly he was quiet — and remained so.

'Mart!' Exmoor's voice was urgent. 'Mart! Speak to me!'

Since there was no response he struggled forward until he found the scientist's hand. Quickly he took the pulse, then let the limp wrist drop from his fingers. There would be no more speaking from Astley — ever.

For a second or two Exmoor was completely bemused. The complete darkness was bewildering: the increasing distant roar a nameless terror. He knew of a thousand things he ought to do. He ought to get to the Protection Squad headquarters — if they still existed — and close this section of the Bore to dam back the approach of waters. He ought to —

He swung round at a faint light from the rear. He met it full on. There were several lamps, swinging in space — the safety lamps of an advance rescue party. Even as he saw them a megaphoned voice called — the unmistakable voice of Lacy, the section foreman.

'Hello there! Hello! Anybody here?'

'Yes — right here!' Exmoor shouted. 'Exmoor calling. Over here! Quickly!'

The lights bobbed and hurried forwards, and against the luminescence great humps and mounds of rock silhouetted themselves. Exmoor got to his feet and went forward at a shambling, unsteady run, until at last he stumbled into the arms of Lacy himself.

'Praise be that you're safe anyway, sir,' Lacy said. 'What about the others? Mr. Astley and those scientific fellows — '

'Wiped out,' Exmoor interrupted. 'I seem to be the only survivor. We've got to hurry and close off this section — The sea's getting through. Can't you hear it?'

Lacy was silent for a moment, his fellow rescuers grouped about him. It did not take long for any of them to detect the ominous noise growing louder with the seconds.

'Come on — out of here,' Exmoor said abruptly. 'We've got to isolate this section of tunnel from Protection Headquarters — '

'But we can't, sir! They're in ruins

160

— shattered by the blast of that explosion. That's why we were so long in coming down here: we had to get the survivors to safety before coming further.'

Exmoor's face was drawn in the torchlight. 'You mean there's no way of sealing off this part of shaft? No way of moving the safety doors?'

'Afraid not, sir. Even if Headquarters hadn't been wrecked, I doubt if the safety doors would move. It's chaos further on, and I'm pretty sure we couldn't move any door in its grooves.'

Exmoor hesitated for a second, trying to decide what to do. But decision was made for him. Suddenly out of the darkness there came a swirl of foaming water, racing round the fallen rocks, gurgling in the dusty floor. Before its onrush the men backed away.

'Out!' Exmoor ordered briefly. 'Nothing for it but to get to the surface.'

He set the example by turning — and at that moment the full deluge came crashing out of the darkness. A foaming, roaring salty flood blasted out of the regions where lay the smashed and

161

transformed neutronium. It swept up the rescue party and Exmoor immediately, bearing them along in a resistless tide in which they fought and struggled for their lives.

They were hurled against rock, bumped against surviving posts of Steel-X, drawn against the rough-edged walls and, at times, were sucked under the waters completely. Lights still operated where the men held onto them because they were waterproof, but they were of little use in the muddy, swirling chaos that surged with ever greater fury into the heart of the shaft.

Exmoor realized one great fact as he battled to save himself. Sooner or later, because of the constantly upward rising of the shaft, there would come a time when the waters would expend their initial fury and, if he could survive that long, he would get through to safety. Everything depended on that: on the gradient being steeper than the inflow of water . . .

So much Exmoor had time to comprehend, then again he was swimming and fighting for his very life, the men around him doing likewise. It seemed they covered miles before they sensed a slackening in the fury of the deluge. The current was not as strong, and the water less deep. There even came a time when at last, exhausted, they could feel Steel-X plates under their feet and they were able to drag themselves clear of the slowly rising waters. They knew they were at some point in the shaft, but exactly where they could not specify.

Lacy dragged himself up behind Exmoor and for a moment they both rested on the crude metalwork, which formed the unfinished edge of the shaft. Lacy's still operative torch waved back into the depths and revealed yellowish rising water flowing out of the mighty shaft.

'This,' Lacy said bitterly, 'looks like the end to me, Mr. Exmoor. We'll never get through now . . . Best thing we can do is get ourselves safe and then try and assess the damage.'

Exmoor nodded moodily, lent a helping hand as more of the rescue party came swimming out of the flood, and then he looked into the distance of the unflooded section of tunnel. The tracks of the small catch-railway were in view going away into darkness, but of course there was no sign of a locomotive or trucks. The catch system itself — a device of projecting levers that aided the train on its steep upward gradient to the main vertical shaft — was out of action.

'We'd better start walking,' Exmoor said. 'There'll be rescue parties at the shaft top, I suppose. Doesn't look as though they're risking coming down here . . . Come on.'

Exmoor started forward, and Lacy followed him. The men who had come out of the flood, and still were coming, followed the example of their boss and so the weary, drenched procession made its way gradually up the mighty upward rise of the shaft. Mile after mile of it, only the torchlights — fortunately everlasting — for company, and behind them the threat of waters that might still overwhelm them.

How far they would have to go none of

them knew. The shaft was 650 miles long, built on a constant slope that would reach its greatest depth at the central rendez-vous — if that glorious goal were ever to be attained. Great sections of the shaft were already lined with Steel-X, but other parts were not yet done for some technical reason or other . . . On the last 3,000 ft of shaft there was a direct vertical climb to the surface.

To tramp 600 miles of shaft — assuming 50 miles had been covered in the floodwater rush — was impossible. Exmoor hoped for one thing: that rescue men or working squads, unaware of what had happened in the remoter reaches of the Bore, would soon be reached. Which raised another question in his mind. He turned to Lacy, tramping heavily beside him.

'Whereabouts were you and the rescue boys when the explosion happened, Lacy?'

''bout a couple of miles back up the shaft, sir. We were sent that far by Mr. Astley for our own safety. We'd have been cleared out altogether like the others if we hadn't preferred to take a gamble.'

'Like the others?' Exmoor repeated.

'Yes, sir. Mr. Astley took it on himself to give orders while you were away from headquarters. He insisted it was safer for all men to be cleared from the tunnel when he smashed that neutronium barrier. Only a few decided to stay and risk it — Steel-X welders, for instance.'

'Yes, I saw them,' Exmoor muttered. 'I'm afraid they've paid for their gamble, too!' He was silent for a moment, tramping steadily. Then he said, 'You realize what this means, Lacy?'

'I think so, sir. That we're not likely to run into any help on the way back.'

'Exactly. That's just the way it looks.'

But in this assumption both men were wrong. It was about an hour later when they heard unexpected sounds — the rattle and clank of the catch railway system! After that it was not long before the fussy little engine itself came into view, trailing wagonloads of eager men armed with every conceivable tool for rescue work. A vast shout of relief went up as Exmoor and Lacy came staggering

166

eagerly out of the tunnel's remoter depths.

'Any more down there, sir?' asked the burly workman in charge of the labour gang.

'A few. You'd better go and look . . . ' Exmoor caught the man's arm as he turned to hurry away. 'Wait a minute! What led you to come and look for us?'

'Instruments, sir. There's a Protection Squad located on the surface, you know.'

'I know, but — You mean their instruments registered the shock of an explosion all that distance away?'

'Seems so, sir.' The man shrugged. 'I'm not up on this scientific racket, but when they told us there'd been a nuclear shock at 600 miles depth I did a bit of thinking, remembering what Mr. Astley had said he was going to do to a neutronium barrier. I figured there might have been an accident so I collected some of the boys and came to look . . . '

'Good man,' Exmoor said, patting the massive shoulder. 'I'll see headquarters knows about your initiative.'

'Thank you, sir. Get into the truck and

have a rest. We'll go and see what others we can find.'

It was only by degrees that Exmoor in particular and everybody in general realized what a disaster had struck the British end of the Bore. The squads of experts rushed to the scene of the flood the moment Exmoor arrived at the surface reported their findings after a precious week had slipped by — and of course, once he had read the analysis of catastrophe, Exmoor laid it before a harassed Douglas Lovelace.

'I'll read this when I have the time,' Lovelace said briefly, taking the documents that Exmoor handed to him. 'Tell me in plain language how we're fixed.'

Exmoor shrugged. 'Two hundred miles of the Bore is now flooded, and the distance is increasing with every hour. All electrical installations in the lower reaches are destroyed — so too are the advance Protection Squad headquarters. Some 150 miles of Steel-X plating has been lost due to the collapse of the rockery. The cost is estimated in billions of pounds.'

Lovelace's face was grey. 'And the

water is still rising, you say?'

'Slowly but surely, sir. That's inevitable until the breach is sealed. We're up against it, D.L., and no mistake. I've worked out plans to put things right, but they're going to put us back maybe two years on progress.'

'All right — let's hear your plans, anyway. I'll have to have something to tell the Bore Corporation when they start raising hell, as they surely will.'

'Only solution is to have deep sea divers seal the rock bed breach with Steel-X. That'll be a long and difficult job, but experienced men could do it if directed by engineers in a bathysphere. It means they'll have to go 8,250 feet down into the Atlantic. The exact spot is being worked out by the G-boys right now. The cost will be tremendous — but it should work. We can't do a thing until we stop the Atlantic pouring into the Bore.'

'Assuming the waters could be dammed back, what then?'

'Then comes the pumping of the Bore — an enormous engineering feat on its own. Normally, it would be an impossible feat, but with nuclear energy and machines to help us we'll do it. The water wouldn't be pumped out in the ordinary way: it'd be changed into its basic constituents — oxygen and hydrogen, which gas would be carried through a pipe system into the ventilator shafts and thence into the atmosphere. That overcomes the difficulty of transporting water. It's easy when it's a gas.'

'This your own idea?' Lovelace asked rather doubtfully.

'Not entirely, sir. I've been consulting some of the physicists. Not all of our physical laboratory men were killed in that neutronium explosion.'

'Mmm . . . ' Lovelace mused for a moment, his steel-trap mouth tight with worry. 'I'm all for these ingenious ideas, Boyd, but the big question is finance. To get that will be as big a fight, as far as I am concerned, as getting the Bore back to normal.'

'I know,' Exmoor said seriously. 'And I sympathize. But unfortunately there's no other way — as you'll see when you've read those reports and recommendations.'

'There's also another thing,' Lovelace went on. 'We're going to be up against it with the labour problem. We promised the various redundant men that they'd be at work again the moment the barrier was blasted: now it looks as though they're further away than ever!'

'Leave them to me,' Exmoor said. 'I'll spin them a story somehow. If they make trouble it will be crushed. There's too much at stake for us to give any freedom to potential troublemakers.'

'All right, I'll leave it to you,' Lovelace said — and on that Exmoor went on his way, far more trouble in his mind than he had dared show. This was the biggest setback the Bore had so far received, and if public faith in the enterprise came to be lost now, no power on earth could get the Bore going again.

The newspaper enemies of the Bore, many of them controlled by foreign enterprise, were not slow in the weeks that followed to vilify the Bore project in every possible way. They cited it as the greatest waste of public money ever known. Their headlines took the tone of

BILLIONS SUNK IN THE ATLAN-
TIC. They sympathized in money and
with words with the thousands of workers
who would not be engaged on the Bore
again for weeks, months, and maybe
years. Why should millions on millions be
sunk on this idiotic project to drive a
tunnel from Canada to Britain?

Boyd Exmoor fought back with everything he had got, but although he took a
tough line — and a logical one — he was
on losing ground. Single-handed, he
could not overcome newspapers, television, and radio sponsored by unfriendly
powers. The few mediums that were
loyally on his side were not enough. And
on top of this there was a powerful
undercurrent that he felt convinced had
its source in the missing Arthur Lovelace.
True, he had no proof of the fact, and
the police force could not lay their hands
on public Nuisance No. 1 — yet Exmoor
still remained convinced he was around
somewhere as a very disquieting influence.

At the Canadian end there was
profound sympathy with the plight of the

British — a fact made clear in every Canadian newspaper, television channel, and radio programme . . . And on the personal side there was Judith, giving all the sympathy she could and reporting progress from time to time. Progress was not so rapid as it had been due to increasing hardness of the rocks under pressure. By mid-March 700 miles had been covered on the Canadian side, and from the look of things the engineers looked like finishing the course with flying colours.

As for Judith herself, she evaded all Exmoor's questions regarding herself. She said she felt well again — even though the televisor plainly showed she was not. Certainly she had not rested up as she had promised. There was just nothing that Exmoor could do about it, and he had far too many problems on his mind to permit of him traveling again to Canada.

Then, towards the end of March there came a change. Douglas Lovelace came at last to the end of his battle with the financial giants and succeeded in getting the necessary grants to enable the flooded

Bore to be drained. It was sweet music in Exmoor's ears and he went to work immediately on the preliminary moves. By the end of the month deep-sea divers and attendant bathysphere scientists holding plans and directions were out in the Atlantic — 600 miles out, fighting storms and spring gales, directing their divers as they set to work to find the breach in the ocean floor.

The world looked on, and wondered if the insanity of man had any end. Exmoor looked on too, with a different vision. Remotely, hazily, he could again see the day when the Bore would be completed and every difficulty overcome ... April, May, June, and July went past and still the divers worked and the engineers directed, nearly 8,000 feet down in the ocean, living in a fantastic world of their own.

The hardest part of the oceanic task was to locate the exact position where the seabed had been pierced. Once this problem was overcome there was the added difficulty of defeating the immense vortices and currents created by the 'plughole' through which the waters were pouring. Incredibly garbed divers, looking like spacemen in their pressure suits, kept unwaveringly at their tasks, handling Steel-X plates and manoeuvering them into position in the bedrock. Once they were in place the task was easier since the weight of waters prevented them moving.

So it went on — a job of welding and boring into bedrock, and with every section tested by instruments. Until finally, by early September, the job was done and the undersea contractors reported that the breach had been sealed . . .

That was all Exmoor was waiting for. In the interval of time whilst the undersea men had been sealing the gap, he had been supervising the construction of machines for converting the sea water into oxygen and hydrogen gas, and thanks to his activities the machines were ready for instant use when he gave the word. At the same time labour armies were at last called into action, and with this occurrence, much of the growling and muttering amongst the malcontents was quashed.

Exmoor did not waste a moment.

Engineers immediately began the electrical process of transforming the waters in the flooded Bore into gas, whence it was carried through the great ventilating systems into the open air and thence mingled with the atmosphere. Nobody could see the gas emanating, but instruments showed it was there, and the natural nitrogen in the atmosphere prevented any possibility of fire whilst the two gases remained as separate elements.

The waters began to drop gradually. The hundreds of miles that had been inundated for so many long months began to appear as a sheet of mud and ooze, which was quickly dried out with nuclear flame throwers following in the wake of the 'gas' machines. Behind these again came the mechanical navvies, as well as human ones with picks and shovels, clearing away the vast carpet of dried-up débris left behind.

By the end of October the mopping-up operation was over. The miles had been regained and not a drop of unwanted water showed itself. Exmoor himself examined the break in the rocks caused by the neutronium expansion, and had it sealed for double security underneath with Steel-X plates; then he pronounced himself ready to drive forward once more — ready to plunge through the rock face into which the one-time neutronium had been converted. His only worry now was that more neutronium might present itself. If that happened he would be in difficulties since Astley and the leading physicists were dead, and the problem might be beyond the present laboratory technicians. However, that was in the future, if at all.

Boring resumed on November 10, some eighteen months after the commencement of the project. The advance offices had been reconstructed, including those of the Protection Squad. The sections of shaft that as yet had not been lined with Steel-X were urgently attended to. Emergency doors were examined to be sure, they would slam into place if instant need demanded.

Babel returned. Sixteen new Astley borers went to work on the rock face. The conveyors kept up their everlasting rattle;

the catch railway puffed and snorted up and down the central track. Everywhere men worked in the blinding light and soaring temperature — and in his office, not far from the main site, Exmoor worked with a song in his heart. The Bore was living again, and would continue to live — until it was finished.

Then towards the middle of November there came disquieting news from the Canadian side — and Judith Saunders was the first to tell it, over the televisor. She plunged straight into the subject one evening when Exmoor had contacted her for his usual progress report.

'There seems to be a jinx on this Bore, Boyd,' the girl said, obvious worry in her eyes. 'No sooner do we get out of one mess than we land in another. This time it's us who's in trouble.'

'To what extent?' Exmoor asked.

'Well, as I've been reporting for some time now, our progress is very slow due to the density of the rock under increasing pressure — and now we've hit up against something which the drills can hardly penetrate. At the present rate our progress is of the order of one mile per week. In the middle of March I reported 700 miles. Now it's mid-November and we've only added about another ten miles to the score. That's pretty terrible.'

'What do your G-men have to say?' Exmoor asked.

'Nothing much. The rock seems to be an amalgam of several things — granite, carbon, tungsten, iron — all of them under terrific pressure at such a depth, which naturally doubles and trebles their hardness. Fortunately the drills haven't been ruined as yet — not as they were in your neutronium trouble . . . ' The girl's face reflected an inner thought. 'I think we'd do better if we blasted. It might be dangerous, but at least we'll get on quicker. I've seen the G-boys' probes on the stuff and it's the amalgam all the way. Well-placed nuclear charges would shift it.'

'And might shift other things too, as I know from my own experience,' Exmoor said anxiously. 'If you want my advice you'll keep on drilling, slow though it may be.'

'Well, from my point of view — Excuse me a moment.' Judith turned aside as the telephone on her desk jangled noisily. Exmoor sat watching her tired, strained face as she listened anxiously. Finally she said, 'Very well, that's the only thing we can do. Link up the televisor so I can watch operations.'

'What now?' Exmoor asked, as she rang off.

'It looks as though the decision has been made for me, Boyd. That was the rock face foreman. He's just reported that the drills won't go any further. They're jammed in the amalgam. Only way out is to use explosives. I've given the okay for that, as you heard.'

'Uh-huh. Do you think I'll be able to see the operation take place? Having had some of the same lark myself I might be able to make a suggestion or two.'

'Could be,' the girl agreed. 'Anyway, you'll see it all on the televisor — if you can spare the time from your own work, that is.'

'Certainly I can. This is all connected with the Bore, isn't it?'

180

'You'll not see me for a while, but you'll hear my voice,' the girl said. 'I'm switching the view. Bye bye for now, Boyd.'

'Goodbye — and take care of yourself. You still look a long way from being a hundred percent to me . . . ' Judith did not respond to this, and after a moment the picture of her disappeared and was replaced by a view of the Canadian rock face, half-naked engineers at work connecting up nuclear charges at the base of the obstruction. They worked exactly to outline, using infinite care, and in between answering telephone calls connected with his own job, Exmoor watched the proceedings with intense interest.

'Any comments, Boyd?' came the girl's voice, presently.

'None at all,' he answered. 'They've done the job exactly as it ought to be done — but for God's sake see that the shaft is cleared for miles around before the charge is fired.'

'It will be. The alarm went out some time ago.' The view faded, and for a while there was nothing but a blank screen.

Exmoor waited; then he sat forward again as Judith's face reappeared. She was seated at her desk as before, her eyes on a telemonitor just outside Exmoor's range of vision.

'The danger area's been cleared,' she explained. 'You'll hear the engineer's voice when the charge is about to be fired.'

'Okay . . . Incidentally, Judy, how far are you from the actual barrier?'

'About ten miles. Like you, my headquarters move forward as the Bore progresses. Why?'

'I'm worried about you — but I don't know why.'

'I'm safe enough. Ten miles is — '

'Area cleared, Miss Saunders,' a voice interrupted through a loud speaker. 'We're ready for firing.'

'Go ahead,' Judith said quietly.

There was a long silence, the girl looking intently into her monitor. Exmoor could do nothing but watch her face — and gradually he saw an expression of horror come into it. He hunched forward urgently.

'Judy! What's the matter?'

She flashed him one look of fear and then sprang to her feet. At the same moment Exmoor's televisor blanked as something at the other end cut off contact. But he did hear the girl screaming frantically against a background of booming explosions.

Then that too ceased and there was an agonising silence.

7

The enemy within

It was only by degrees that the full disastrous news reached Exmoor — and the world. At first his frantic 'phonings to Canada brought no satisfactory answer; then gradually the news came that the Canadian end of the Bore was in chaos. The nuclear explosion had penetrated the amalgam rock all right, but it had also done something else — opened up a deep and highly active volcanic seam.

Horrified, the whole world listened to or read of the story of the Bore at the Canadian end being deluged with molten lava and volcanic fire. Thousands of workers had been killed, machines destroyed, and hundreds of miles of progress lost. This in itself would have been bad enough, but there was worse to come. Canada itself was shaken by a vast earthquake, which produced enormous damage throughout

Quebec and razed several buildings in Quebec City itself, Montreal, and Ottawa. The tremors were felt as far westward as Alberta and as far north as the Melville Peninsula. Probably even greater disaster would have occurred had not the pent-up volcanic forces found outlet in an upthrusting new volcanic island to the south of Greenland in the Atlantic Ocean. Here the newborn volcano blasted and roared with unimaginable fury, producing a tremendous rain of ashes and sulphuric smoke for an area of a hundred miles around.

The moment he heard of the disaster Exmoor went immediately to Canada, not only to inquire after Judith of whom the news was sketchy, but also to find out the extent of the damage and how long it would be before boring could resume once more.

Apart from the things he glimpsed on his air flight, which were bad enough in all conscience, Exmoor grasped the real magnitude of the catastrophe when his plane touched down at the new Hopedale airfield. From here, as on the other occasion when he had visited Labrador, it should have been possible to see the mushroom city around the Bore entrance. Instead there was nothing but ruin, an army of labourers at work trying to remove débris and rebuild shattered buildings. It looked, on the face of it, as though the Canadian end of the Bore was dead . . . horribly and completely dead, cremated by an outburst of Nature, which the hand of probing man had released.

Exmoor talked with officials in hastily reconstructed offices; he talked with foremen and technicians, and all of them seemed to have come to the same conclusion — that as far as Canada was concerned this was the finish.

And Judith? It seemed that she was in hospital, recovering from injuries sustained at the time of the explosion. Once he had the rather garbled facts from the men in charge, Exmoor hurried on to visit her in the big, still-standing hospital on the outskirts of Hopedale. Originally built when the mushroom town had been constructed, it was now filled to capacity with injured workers from the Bore — Judith amongst them.

He did not go immediately to Judy; he sought out first the physician in charge of her case, a matter-of-fact and obviously overworked medico by the name of Dr. Malpin.

'You realize my concern, doctor,' Exmoor continued, when he had got through the preliminaries. 'Miss Saunders is the technical Engineer-in-Charge of the enterprise on this side of the ocean. I must have some assurance of when she will be able to continue her activities.'

The medico hesitated and looked seriously at Exmoor over his glasses.

'I have every right to know,' Exmoor insisted. 'Both from the business and personal side. I am Miss Saunders' fiancé, you know.'

'Yes — so I believe . . . Naturally, you would wish me to be frank?'

'Naturally.'

'Very well, then. I am sorry, Mr. Exmoor, but I don't see any possibility of Miss Saunders returning to her duties on the Bore — granting the project is continued with. She will never be able undertake work of that nature again.'

'I hadn't realised,' Exmoor said slowly, searching Malpin's face, 'that she is so badly injured.'

'She isn't. A broken arm and crushed ribs as a result of the volcanic explosion. That is the main extent.'

'Then — then why can't she return to work?'

'Because it would hasten her . . . death.' Malpin spoke with intense seriousness. 'I'm sorry to have to tell you this, but you asked for me to be frank.'

'Yes — of course,' Exmoor said mechanically.

'Miss Saunders is incurably ill,' Malpin sighed. 'We found that out when she was brought in here after the explosion. Had she sought advice earlier her complaint might have been cured — or at least alleviated. Now, unhappily, it is too late.'

'But what is the *matter* with her?' Exmoor demanded.

'She's suffering from an advanced form of radioactivated disease — something like cancer. To cut a long story short she went to work in the Bore too soon after her father had a barrier blown up with nuclear explosives. She was affected seriously by the fallout remains, even though at the time she was probably not aware of it. There have been dozens of cases of workers similarly affected at that time; they sought advice, but she did not. Therein lies the tragedy.'

Exmoor gazed fixedly at the desk. 'Has she been told?'

'No. One hesitates to tell a person that they are doomed. If she asks the question direct she will be told; not otherwise.'

'This explains so much,' Exmoor muttered. 'Her tiredness, her mysterious emotional breakdowns, her almost frantic desire to get the Bore finished — Just as if she might know somehow that she hasn't long to do it in.'

The medico nodded slowly. 'Maybe she does know instinctively; impending death has a way of forcing itself on the consciousness. However, she cannot return to work; apart from the disease with which she is afflicted there must be further nuclear fallout danger in the Bore now following the recent explosion. She will not work on the Bore again, Mr. Exmoor, and believe me when I say I am truly sorry.'

'The Bore has something of the quality of Frankenstein's monster, don't you think?' Exmoor whispered. 'What will it take from us next?'

'I beg your pardon?' Malpin frowned a little.

'Nothing, doctor — just a thought. Tell me, how long do you think Miss Saunders has?'

'Maybe a year at the outside, with proper care. Maybe less. Radioactive disease is an illness on which prognoses are difficult.'

'I understand. Thanks very much for the information. I'd like to see Judith, if I may?'

'Certainly. There is no question of any infection, you understand. Injections have negated that risk.'

Within a few minutes Exmoor found himself in the private room that had been allotted to the girl. It was cool and quiet and there was a faint perfume from the vase of flowers near the bed. Exmoor went forward, smiling, trying to forget everything he had been told. The girl smiled back at him, her right arm in splints and bandages, and her ribs showing a bulky binding beneath her nightdress. Her slightly greying black hair was wearily lank and her grey eyes too big for her face.

'Hello, Boyd!' Her voice was extremely low as she held out her sound hand to welcome him.

'A bright one you are!' he joked, kissing her. 'Cracking your ribs and opening up a volcanic seam! What have you got to say for yourself, young lady?'

'All I can say is: it could have happened to anybody.'

'You're right,' Exmoor agreed seriously. 'Horribly right. I never saw such a shambles in all my life . . . Maybe you've seen it too by now?'

Judith nodded. 'Only a televisor.' She glanced towards it on a nearby table. 'I don't think you know the half of it, Boyd. This damage has turned the public against us. The earthquake was a pretty terrible business, you know.'

'I do know. I've come over to get the facts, and see you. The technicians say the Bore won't carry on from this side.'

'I've heard that rumour too.' A strained look came over the girl's pale face. 'In that case, Boyd, everything father fought for — everything I've fought for — is lost. Even if Britain finishes the job it won't be the same. Dad's ambition was to get to the central rendezvous, and when he died his ambition became mine.'

'Yes . . . I know.' Exmoor deliberately lost himself in thought, from which he had to arise as the girl spoke again.

'Once I'm on my feet again I'll very soon make myself heard in the right quarter. I know there's been terrible damage, but none of it is a dead stop to our progress. The Bore isn't even flooded. Thanks to the magma that flowed from the seam, it cooled as it flowed and sealed up any possible openings through which the sea could penetrate. The worst part will be shifting the now solidified volcanic matter, which is blocking the Bore. The drills will make short work of that . . . I've been planning it all out whilst I've been lying here.'

Exmoor smiled faintly. 'I'll bet you have! Never once given yourself a chance to relax and recover your strength, have you?'

'I'm not interested in that. My life is the Bore, and I must see it completed . . . somehow.'

'Suppose — just suppose,' Exmoor said uncomfortably, 'that you don't go back into action for a long time? Suppose you feel more groggy than you anticipated; have you anybody who can do the work for you until you're really fit?'

'Not now. There were quite a few good men who were like my right hand, but they all died in the volcanic seam explosion. I'm the only one who knows what's wanted. I'll do it, too . . . ' The girl paused for a moment, giving Exmoor an odd look. 'What do you mean — if I feel more groggy than I anticipate? There's nothing about crushed ribs and a broken arm that can't be put right, is there?'

'Nothing, dear,' Exmoor agreed quietly. 'Nothing at all.'

Silence. Exmoor stirred slightly on the small chair at the bedside; then he leaned forward and cupped the girl's hand in his big palms.

'Judy, this may be a queer sort of time, in the midst of a man-sized catastrophe as far as you're concerned, but — why don't we get married? Why don't you let me legally shoulder a lot of your responsibilities? Why wait until the Bore's finished? The way things are, that ten year limit doesn't look so cockeyed after all.'

Judy turned her face away on the pillow. 'I'm sorry, Boyd, but since you've brought the subject up I may as well speak. I — I don't want to marry you.'

'You — you don't want? But we're engaged, aren't we?'

'Yes, but we did that in rather a hurry. Didn't think about it. I was going to tell you at an opportune moment that we'd be better — separate. When we got engaged the Bore was only a part of my life and dad was still alive. Now it's all my life! You must have noticed how — how distant I've been. Noticed the change in me since I took over control.'

'Only because you were — and still are — run down.'

Judith said nothing but her shoulders quivered. Abruptly Exmoor forced her to look at him. Her eyes were full of tears.

'If our engagement means nothing, why do you cry?' he asked gently.

'Because — because I don't want to drag you down with me,' Judith gasped, in the midst of another of her emotional outbursts. 'Why can't you understand? Why? Why should a strong, healthy man like you chain himself up to me? Can't you understand, Boyd? Understand the real reason for my apparent look of interest in you these past months? I . . . I haven't got above a few months to live! That's why!'

'I know that — but I don't believe it,' Exmoor said seriously, still hanging onto her hand.

She stared through her tears. 'You know? But how could you? I never told anybody that I'm poisoned with radioactivity; I found it out for myself by various tests I made for myself.'

'And failed to seek advice.'

'It had gone too far when I discovered what was wrong with me. Boyd, how do you know?'

'You don't expect to come into a

hospital without them finding out all about you, do you? Dr. Malpin told me, if you must know — But none of it makes any difference. I still love you, and I know you must certainly love me else you wouldn't have tried such a crazy way of trying to cool me off! We're going to marry, my dearest, and fight whatever trouble there is between us.'

'But, Boyd, you have so much on your hands. You can't afford to have a wife who — '

'My wife is the woman I love, and that's all that concerns me. You're not going to die, dearest; you're going to see your ideal come true, and live to enjoy it through the years . . . and years.'

Judith did not say any more. In fact she could not. She dissolved, sobbing gently, into Exmoor's arms as he leaned across the bed.

★   ★   ★

Exmoor was a man of action. Before he left Canada, two days later, he had married Judy by special license and departed with the promise to be back as soon as ever possible. Maybe within a week, when he had consulted with the British end of the Bore Corporation. He knew, very clearly, that there was much to be done. Canada was on the brink of outlawing the Bore forever under the pressure of public opinion, and with the girl unable to speak for herself Exmoor realized that it was up to him to get something done.

First he checked on the British activities and made sure all was going well; then, leaving a responsible deputy in charge he sought out Douglas Lovelace in London and argued matters out with him. Though he was, of course, responsible to the entire Bore Corporation for every move he made, he nevertheless had a great deal of personal influence with Canadian and British high-ups.

'The business devolves on you, D.L.,' Exmoor insisted, when he had outlined the details of the Canadian debacle. 'You're head of the project, and so you have the most influence. Only you can talk the Canadian Government into seeing eye-to-eye with you. If you don't, you can write the Canadian enterprise off as a dead loss and we'll be left with completing the Bore from the British end alone. That will double our time and we'll be perhaps twenty years finishing the job! Even at that we might not do it, especially if the Canadian Government refuses to allow the project to go through.'

'What's your candid opinion?' Lovelace asked. 'You've seen Government men whilst over there — and the extent of the disaster. How do we stand?'

'In pretty bad odour, I'm afraid. Three Canadian cities have been partially wrecked, and there's been an enormous amount of other damage from earthquake shocks. We'd have the devil of a bill on top of us except for the fact that our own lawyers have swung an 'Act of God' clause, claiming — successfully — that the opening of the volcanic seam was not deliberate, but could have happened to anybody. 'Act of God' has saved us on that score. But . . . '

'But what?'

'We're up against the temper of the

Canadian people, which is being made all the sharper by the agents in their midst. Our enemies are working overtime, believe me — just as they did in England when we had that Bore flood. The Canadian people are demanding that the Bore be shut down at their end. They've got to be talked out of it — or at least the Government has. They are neutral, simply spokesmen for the people.'

'Right. I'll see what I can do,' Lovelace muttered, thinking. 'There's only one thing worries me: since, so you say, Miss Saunders won't be carrying on who's to take control in her place? The present technicians are all against us, aren't they?'

'I'm afraid they are.' Exmoor reflected for a moment. 'There's only one thing for it — if they can't find anybody willing or reliable enough I'll do it myself. I'll direct both ends and delegate a lot of the British work to Anderson. He's a good man and he's deputising for me at this very moment.'

'You're going to take the devil of a load on your back,' Lovelace warned, 'but I suppose even that risk is better than closing the Bore down after the money that's been poured into it . . . Okay, Boyd, I'll leave for Canada immediately.'

★ ★ ★

As Exmoor returned to take over the British control, Douglas Lovelace entered into his battle with the Canadian government. It was towards the end of November when he opened the preliminary proceedings, reinforced by members of the Bore Corporation whom he knew would be favourable towards his cause. It was mid-January the following year before he gained what he wanted. Ahead of him paraded a vast propaganda campaign to offset the damaging rumours and suggestions of the unfriendly elements — a campaign so well conducted that the Canadian people came to believe that the real tragedy would be in stopping the Bore instead of continuing with it. Their own money, in the shape of taxes, was locked up indirectly in the project, for which there had to be a financial return. Unless they carried on they wouldn't get it. In fact they'd have heavier taxes, with no reward, due to the cost of filling in the shaft that had already been dug. In fact the essence of the propaganda was nothing but clever mumbo-jumbo, but it had the desired effect. The decision was reached: the Canadian end of the Bore would continue, and to this end men and machines were drafted back again to the frozen wilderness of Labrador's winter to commence anew the struggle.

During this time Exmoor had not come up against any trouble. He seemed to have things on an even keel again. He was now 800 miles forward, and at a depth of approximately 10,000 feet. True, as it had been in Canada, progress was slowed up by the terrific hardness of the rock under pressure, but serious snags did not seem to present themselves, even though he was ready for them. The biggest shock he got was when he knew Judith was going to direct the Canadian end as before. The name of a new controller had been suppressed from the news, but Lovelace himself did not seem to be in any doubt about it.

'Has Judy gone crazy?' Exmoor demanded, striding angrily around Lovelace's office. 'She isn't *fit* to do it, D.L. She told me so herself, and so did the doctor.'

'That's as maybe,' Lovelace shrugged. 'Towards the end of my negotiations with the Canadian government she took part in the proceedings. I agree that she didn't look well, but all her determination was there. The moment she knew you were going to try and handle both ends she insisted that she should resume her former work. And I don't think I have to tell you, Boyd, that when your wife says a thing she means it.'

'Why hasn't it been in the papers, or on the television, that she's back on the job?' Exmoor snapped.

'Because of the prejudice against her. The public still feels that a woman can't do the job properly, though we know she can. She's blamed entirely for that volcanic eruption. It seemed a good idea to keep her name out of things once we'd come to an agreement. It'll creep out gradually that she's at work again.'

'I still think she's crazy,' Exmoor

muttered. 'Just wait until I have words with her on the television.'

'That's up to you,' Lovelace said. 'But for God's sake don't shout too loud. We've had enough trouble as it is.'

Exmoor merely grunted something and then, after he had finished numerous business details, he took his departure. Once he was back in his advance office he put through a direct telecall to the Labrador end — and presently Judith's face merged on the screen.

'Why hello, Boyd! I wasn't expecting a call from you until the usual progress report this evening . . . There isn't anything wrong, is there?'

'As a matter of fact, I think there's a good deal wrong, Judy! I've just heard from D.L. that you're taking over the Canadian control again! What on earth are you trying to do? You know it's a fatal mistake in your condition.'

Judith smiled faintly. 'There are two aspects to the matter, Boyd. One is that I might as well be hung for a sheep as a lamb, and the other is that you're not a superman.'

'Meaning what?' Exmoor asked. He was studying the girl meanwhile and reflecting to himself that the enforced rest in hospital had done her good. Though she still did not look really well, she was certainly better than before.

'Meaning that, in regard to the second matter, you can't possibly control both the British and Canadian ends and do both properly. The strain will be too much and you'll go under.'

Exmoor's belligerent expression softened a little. 'So that's it. You're doing it to help me?'

'Of course — and the project on which we're working. You don't think — no matter what the consequences — that I can sit around in cotton wool waiting for the end, do you? Besides, you said yourself that I was going to see my ideal come true and live to enjoy through years and years.'

'I still believe that, dearest,' Exmoor said simply. 'Only to see you working again in the Bore, and knowing what medical opinion says — '

'Never mind medical opinion. They're

not always correct. If I'm to die I may as well do it while I'm busy. Besides, you must have help — and that's where a good wife takes her stand.'

'But not in peril of your own life, Judy!'

'It's my own life, Boyd — and I'm sure the Almighty won't punish me for trying to be of help.'

'I'll say no more,' Exmoor said quietly. 'I always knew you were a woman of extraordinary courage — and now I'm sure of it. But I'll watch over you night and day.'

'You also have a job to do, Boyd. Never forget that.'

There was a resolute finality about the girl's tone, and Exmoor did not try to argue against it. He found it simpler to change the subject entirely.

'We may as well call this a progress report and so justify the expense of the telecall, Judy. I have to report that all goes well as far as we're concerned. We're about 10,000 feet down now. How's things with you?'

'We were advancing quite well when disaster struck us. Our present estimate is that 300 miles of tunnel is clear and the men are at work blasting away amalgam and rubbish from the eruption. So, technically, we're at a standstill, but we'll soon get organized again . . . And we'll still meet at the central rendezvous as Mr. and Mrs. Bore Project,' the girl smiled.

'Bless you,' Exmoor said, his lips forming a kiss. 'Bless you for your courage and for marrying me.'

'One can look at that both ways,' Judith answered seriously; then she became practical again. 'That's all for now, Mr. Exmoor. I'll be here when next you call.'

Exmoor switched off, meditated for a moment or two, and then turned back to his work — but he could not concentrate on it. He could not rid himself of the thought that Judith, whom he loved so much, was deliberately taking the risk of shortening her threatened life span by working once more in the Bore. He abruptly found himself cursing the fates — cursing the blight that had descended on the girl. Somewhere, somehow, in these scientific days, there ought surely to be a cure? Yet apparently not. Had not

Dr. Malpin himself denied such a possibility?

Exmoor sighed and forced attention back to his work, wishing that more of his heart were in it. Then he suddenly realized how much Judith was sacrificing in order that the tunnel might progress. And with the realization came self-reproach. If she could do good work with the ever-present threat of extinction hanging over her, surely he could with no physical handicap?

That was enough for Exmoor. From that moment onward he never once relaxed, never once questioned whether the Bore was worthwhile. He worked incessantly, stopping only for sleep, meals, and a daily communication with Judith.

The weeks grew into months. The drills drove on relentlessly. Back now through 900 miles of Bore the gleaming, satiny walls and curving roof of Steel-X spread, making the tunnel seem like the inside of a highly polished cannon. Men were everywhere, working with good heart now nothing seemed to be going wrong. The temperature was 116°, and even the draft from the ventilating system was as hot as the Italian sirocco, but nobody complained. By now the heat, the din, and the glaring light were part of life itself, part of the price that had to be paid for building this immaculate engineering vista, which spread behind.

June, year two of the Project. Canada had got started again. Judith reported that the original distance of 710 miles had been reached, and was now rapidly being surpassed. The geologists had inspected the volcanic seam and found its actual source to be well below the point where the future Bore would extend. In any event there was no danger now since all volcanic pressure was expending itself through the new active volcano at the foot of Greenland. The drills were in action again, gnawing their way through granite, gneiss, marble, carbon, and tungsten. Labour poured into the job; millions on millions of dollars were sacrificed before this undersea Moloch gradually creeping towards its destination at the central rendezvous.

Then again trouble struck — on the British side, and this time Exmoor was on the spot when it happened. He was in the midst of checking specifications at the rock face, foreman Lacy beside him. Both men had half an eye to the screaming tune of the sixteen huge drills nearby — and abruptly the unexpected happened.

They both swung round appalled as all sixteen drills, working in a horizontal line with each other to obtain simultaneity of boring, crashed their needle-snouts into something as soft as treacle. It gushed out from sixteen holes; then just as quickly the entire rock face gave way, already extremely friable from the drilling it had received.

So much Exmoor and Lacy had time to notice; then the treacle flood hurled them off their feet. Table and specifications vanished in a syrupy smother. Men fought to swim in the heavy substance. Gangs of labourer's further back, hesitated and then started to run.

'It's oil!' Lacy gasped frantically, as Exmoor fought beside him. 'One devil of a gusher! Maybe an inner sea of oil.'

Exmoor nodded, but he had too much on his mind to say anything. He fought his way through the stuff, feeling like a fly swimming in a can of molasses. Further up the tunnel, since the deluge did not travel very rapidly, the tunnel was clear. Further away still — a mile perhaps — was a safety door that could be swung across. Exmoor realized he had got to get there, somehow.

But the Protection Squad in their perched-up offices was ahead of him. They had already seen what was coming and actuated the levers that swung the door across. Still Exmoor swam on, the high searchlights illuminating every move. Glancing back he could see men struggling in the filth, some going under, some climbing onto tall machines — Then came real horror.

Abruptly the oil flood caught alight! How it happened Exmoor did not know. Perhaps a fused wire — perhaps anything. All he knew was that a livid wall of dancing flame, belching thick black smoke, was flashing towards him. He winced and then shouted with the pain as flames leapt over his head and arms. To save himself he deliberately dived deep into the oil itself, which to a great extent saved him since the flames were on the surface only as yet.

In this way, choked and racked with pain, he swam the rest of the distance to where the oil flood ended and staggered out of the flaming hell with his shirt burned away and the skin of his arms peeling. His eyebrows had gone, but his hair — under the steel helmet strapped under his chin — had survived.

Half blind with anguish he reeled his way up the tunnel and shouted hoarsely as he reached the huge safety door. He looked back and saw Lacy following him — a burned, stumbling wreck of a man kept on his feet by sheer willpower. In the further distance men were screaming and vanishing in the blazing sea. And one man in particular seemed to be watching it all with an unnatural calm. He was perched on the top of a mechanical navvy, surveying. Somehow he looked like —

The safety door slid back a fraction.

Instantly Exmoor squirmed through it. It closed. Then it reopened to permit Lacy through. So it went on — one by one, but Exmoor was struggling up the steps into the Protection Squad offices. The staff gazed at him in silent wonder as he came in — blackened, oil-caked, red weals showing on his arms.

'Keep — keep the section closed!' he ordered the official in charge. 'These flames have got to burn themselves out.'

'But there may be survivors, Mr. Exmoor — '

'Do as you're told!' Exmoor snapped. 'A few survivors can cost us everything — The whole Bore could go up in smoke if those flames get through.'

The staff became grimly silent, watching the blazing oil below. All of it was ignited now, and where there were any survivors they were overtaken at the oil's edge and died like ants on a griddle.

Weakly, holding on to instruments at the edge of the bench, Exmoor dragged himself forward to look. His eyes moved up at once to the solitary man on the navvy. He was still watching.

212

'There are a few men round the door, sir,' the charge hand ventured. 'Have I still to keep it closed?'

Exmoor looked at them, a huddle of half a dozen, hammering on the great barrier and then looking back in terror at the crawling sea of flame creeping nearer to them.

'All right — snap it open for them,' Exmoor said abruptly. 'Then close it again. And keep it that way.'

'Right, sir.' The door opened and shut. The released men went staggering into the protected length of tunnel, into the arms of labourers and technicians who had gathered there for safety — and to watch the proceedings.

Exmoor looked about him, breathing hard. The view was relatively clear since the belching smoke from the oil fire was being drawn away by the ventilating system, otherwise suffocation would have been a very real peril.

'Thank God for these safety doors — and this one in particular,' Exmoor muttered at last. 'Otherwise the whole Bore would have gone. There are countless explosives stored — plenty of timber, oil and petrol dumps . . . ' He stopped, wincing with pain. 'How did this lot catch alight? That's what I can't understand.'

His eyes rose abruptly to the man on the mechanical navvy. Flames were all around him now. Abruptly Exmoor snatched the microphone to him and switched it on. His voice boomed through the high-up amplifying system.

'There's nothing we can do for you, friend! You should have gone with the others — not climb up that damn' thing!'

The man's voice yelled back, audible through the pickup speakers. 'I'll die with only one regret, Exmoor — that I didn't set the whole Bore alight! I nearly made it, but you were a bit too quick with that door!'

'Arthur Lovelace!' Exmoor exclaimed. 'I thought I knew that figure, but somehow the face seemed different . . . '

Though he only muttered the words the amplifiers picked them up clearly, and brought a crazy laugh from the isolated Lovelace.

'Of course you didn't recognise me! Neither did anybody else when I rejoined this labour corps. I had my face fixed in Europe by plastic surgeons . . . Curse you and your pestilential tunnel, Exmoor! I was waiting for an accident like this, and I was quick to take advantage of it. I was near the safety lamps when the oil gushed. I dropped two of them into it, lighted — their gauze masks smashed up. Easy to do with so much rock about . . .'

Exmoor waited, the rest of the staff listening intently.

'What about the rest of the lamps, sir?' one of the men asked urgently, staring at the surviving lamps high on the rock face, glowing dimly yellow above the flames.

'Can't make any difference now,' Exmoor said. 'In any case they wouldn't have ignited anything due to the gauze perforations being so small . . .' He banged his fist suddenly on the bench beside him.

'But for this swine deliberately breaking two — '

'All right, I can hear you!' Lovelace yelled. 'I've failed this time, but there will be others — hundreds of them — who'll take my place — who'll work for those who say the Bore should never be built — '

Lovelace stopped with a scream of pain as a fire tongue shot the length of the navvy. Exmoor jerked his head away. When he looked again Arthur Lovelace had gone and the navvy was a dim skeleton amidst the raging fire.

'Are we going to be safe here, sir?' the staff charge-hand asked anxiously. 'The fire's getting worse.'

Exmoor looked at it grimly. 'And will do as long as oil flows. We'll be safe here because we're just beyond the safety door even though we can see over the top of it. Contact the surface fire department and have them do what they can with foam extinguishers, though I imagine it'll be precious little. I'll contact the emergency drilling section and see if something can't be done to stop the oil. It's valuable, once this residue has burned out . . . '

There was a whole lot more that Exmoor intended to say, but suddenly the pain of his burns, which he had grimly been trying to ignore up to now, became too much for him. He had a recollection of the floor rising up to hit him . . . and that was all.

8

The final peril

In a few hours Exmoor was about again. Strong drinks, an iron constitution, and hospital treatment made quick work of patching him up. Then he returned promptly to the scene of the disaster to find that, contrary to his expectations, the fire brigade had succeeded in snuffing out the blaze. Thousands of gallons of foam were still pouring on the dying oil flames over the top of the emergency door when Exmoor arrived. He spent only a few moments with the fire chief and then hurried into the Protection Squad offices to survey the setup.

The oil, still burning in sections, had raised its level considerably and was now approximately five feet deep and still pouring through the shattered rock face. From the midst of the oil, the deserted drills and mechanical navvies protruded themselves like islands, their metalwork blackened with smoke, but otherwise undamaged.

Exmoor turned finally and picked up the 'phone. In a matter of moments he was speaking to the head of the Emergency Drilling Section on the surface, a unit maintained as an auxiliary to the main Boring Units, and normally engaged on the welding and positioning of Steel-X plates.

'Bill?' Exmoor questioned, as a voice answered. 'Exmoor here. Get your men together — we've a job to do down at the rock face. Make it quick, and bring all your gear.'

'I've heard about the oil fire, sir,' the engineer said. 'Would it have anything to do with that?'

'It certainly would! I'll explain when you come — and hurry it up.'

'Right, sir.'

Exmoor put the 'phone down and looked again at the multitude of pipes leading back to the foam pumping engines. He surveyed the black, syrupy oil — then turned sharply as a voice spoke.

'What are the next moves, chief?' It was foreman Lacy who asked the question — bandaged about the face and right eye but otherwise looking as tough as ever.

'Glad to see you're still on your feet, Lacy,' Exmoor smiled.

'And rarin' to go, sir. What do I do with all these loafers in the tunnel? They're just standing around exchanging yarns, which is no way to get a Bore constructed!'

'There'll be plenty of work for them before long. I've just phoned Bill of the emergency drilling section. I want him — and you — to help me cap that oil gusher.'

'Okay, boss . . . ' Lacy looked at the syrupy flood. 'We sure run into some stuff, don't we, boss? Worst thing about that oil was it catching fire as it did. From the checkup I've made it cost us nearly a hundred men.'

'You know why it caught fire, don't you?' Exmoor asked sharply.

'No idea. I was too busy getting free of it and then having myself patched up.'

'It was Arthur Lovelace's work . . . '

Exmoor gave the details as Lacy stared at him in grim fury. 'And before he died he said there'd be others. Which I don't doubt for a moment. From here on, Lacy, tighten up your vigilance and try as near as you can to discover the records of the men working for us — particularly on the rock face. The end of Lovelace junior isn't the end of trouble, I'm afraid.'

With that Exmoor let the matter drop. Turning to the 'phone again he was soon talking to Douglas Lovelace on the direct line to London.

'Boyd Exmoor speaking, D.L. I'm afraid we've run into fresh trouble, but it isn't so big that we'll be stuck for long. In a word, we've accidentally struck oil — with disastrous results.' Exmoor gave every detail and then finished, 'But for the safety door being closed in time the whole Bore might have been ablaze. And there's only one person to thank for it — your son!'

'Arthur!' Lovelace exclaimed. 'But I thought he — '

'Thought he was out of harm's way? So did all of us. I'm afraid he pursued his crackpot notions to the last, his face remodeled by a plastic surgeon . . . I'm not going to harp on his wrong motives, D.L., or his dangerous activity. I'm just telling you that we know now where he is . . . He's dead.'

There was a long silence as the industrialist presumably absorbed the news and then mastered himself. When he did at last speak again his voice was coldly businesslike.

'What are your next moves going to be, Boyd? I don't have to remind you that oil's a valuable contribution to the money side of our efforts, do I?'

'I'd already thought of that, sir. The fire's about dead now. Once it's finally out I'm going to lead a party of engineers to seal off the oil; then we can get started again when we've removed what remains of bodies. I'll have to discuss with you personally a means of getting the oil to the surface.'

'I'll expect you the moment you can manage it.'

'One last thing, sir — keep this business as quiet as possible. I'll instruct everybody here to keep their mouths shut. We've had enough bad publicity without any more — and this is a setback which can soon be mastered, anyway.'

★ ★ ★

Altogether, the hold-up progress on the British end of the Bore lasted a month, and during that month Exmoor and his team of engineers and helpers worked almost the twenty-four hours round the clock. The difficult job was not to cap the source of the oil flow, but to find it. They floated on an improvised raft in the mighty caverns beyond the crumbled rock face, risking their lives every moment they were at work. Until they finally came to realize that this was a vast inner oil sea, and that their only chance lay in building the Bore across it, on Steel-X foundations, whilst the oil-sea itself must be pumped to the surface.

So, after the month had been absorbed in investigation and surface-negotiation there were two teams at work in the depths — one building the Bore across the oil sea, on pillars and plates of Steel-X, and the others constructing the mighty pipe lines which were to carry the precious oil to the surface where a refinery was already in rapid construction. At least the Bore itself would be safe — Exmoor and the geologists were satisfied on this. The pillars were embedded in rock beneath the oil and, as such, were completely immovable.

Advance began once more, on the opposite side of the oil sea. Once more the ponderous masses of the Astley drills nosed and ate their way through the rock; once more the mechanical navvies and conveyors got to work, and the thousands of labourers and technicians went back to their gruelling occupations under the watchful eye of foreman Lacy.

Exmoor, as far as his burns went, was practically himself again. In any case he had never missed a daily communication with Judy, and he had never mentioned his injuries either. The month's hold-up he had simply explained away as a sea of oil, which solution the girl had readily accepted. She knew nothing of the machinations of Lovelace junior, nor for that matter did anybody else. The matter had been hushed up completely.

Canada, the girl reported, had now bored to 950 miles and a depth of 11,000 feet. So far, no holdups. She looked well enough despite her activities and the physical trouble weighing her down. It seemed pretty obvious to Exmoor that the sheer thrill of doing what she wanted to do was keeping Judith up to scratch. He began to wonder how she would react when the boring was ended. Would reaction catch up all at once, or what?

For his own part he could report that the first 1,000 miles had been covered which left only 250 miles to go to the central rendezvous. And the way ahead, as far as the geologists could judge, was comparatively free.

1,000 miles! 1,000 miles through the earth in the shape of a flattened 'U'. A depth of 12,000 feet! Deliberately, Exmoor gave the order to slow down. Not unreasonably, he felt that the men had earned a brief respite and the chance to see their families once again. He gave the order that work would cease for three days once Canada also reported 1,000 miles. There would be a celebration in the depths — a celebration before the final conquest when the two opposing ends of Bore would meet.

It came about exactly as Exmoor had visualized. By mid-September Canada had reached the 1,000-mile mark in one tremendous forward drive m which no snags occurred. At that point, by mutual consent, work halted. It was a pause that had the blessing of the Bore Corporation too, since it enabled the hard-worked staff to also take three days off, a pause in the midst of a summer nearly ended.

With a skeleton staff left in charge to keep a watchful eye on things, Exmoor came to the surface — out of those polished, Steel-X galleries which, at last, loomed as a forecast of what the whole Bore would eventually be like. Smooth, immaculate, perfect, the greatest engineering feat ever attempted.

On the surface, in Bore City — as the mushroom town around the Land's End opening was called — a gigantic feast and celebration was arranged to mark the first 1,000 miles, but Exmoor himself did not attend. He gave his good wishes through Lacy and then took a strato-liner to Canada.

There, for three perfect days and nights, they became a natural husband and wife, newly weds indeed, and the Bore hardly entered their discussions. They walked together in the autumnal countryside, they visited theatres, they spent the nights in the big hotel which Exmoor had booked before he had left England. For all too brief a time they snatched at something of normalcy, knowing all too well that before long the Bore would claim them for the final plunge.

It did. The three days were gone all too soon as Exmoor was flying back across the Atlantic, wonderfully refreshed for the break and yet with a cloud on his mind . . . Judith was failing. He had seen it in her manner, in her curious listlessness, in her make-believe efforts to seem sublimely happy. Relentlessly, mercilessly, the disease that had her in its grip was making terrible inroads, even more so now that she was back in the inhospitable atmosphere of the Bore.

'Two hundred and fifty miles for each of us,' Exmoor mused to himself, as the plane hurtled the ocean. 'Not far. She'll last that long — then whatever else comes she must get away to fresh air, rest, new surroundings . . . She can't, she mustn't, die after all we've been through.'

Proud, defiant words. That he knew — but somehow there was a deep feeling within him that for once he might cheat the Bore. Perhaps it wouldn't take everything. If it did, where was the glory and reward for having built it . . . ?

Of necessity, once he returned to the site, Exmoor had to put Judith out of his mind, just as she had to put him out of hers. There was a multitude of things to do, by both of them — and first of all came the check-up with the geologists for 'tunnel straightness' How far, in the 1,000 miles each side, had the Bore diverged from the central rendezvous? Soundings were taken, the latest geologic findings taken from both sides, and the results pooled. They proved encouraging. So far as could be ascertained the two ends would meet almost exactly at the theoretical central rendezvous. There was no more than 20 feet of divergence off-centre, which said a great deal for the precision of the engineering.

Exmoor went ahead with high hopes. The greatest depths under the Atlantic were now being reached, and would end at a maximum of 12,500 feet. He wished Martin Astley could be here to see this final drive, to watch his superb drills tearing the heart out of the pressured rock and driving ever forward in the whining, screaming Babel which had become a part of every man's life down here in the depths.

The second year of the project — October — November — December. Vast pressure and a slowing down of progress. January, year three — Britain 1,100 miles and 12,100 feet depth. Canada — practically the same.

Three months to move 100 miles. It was as if the resisting earth was trying everything in order to prevent a final victory. Pressure, pressure, always pressure — the ever increasing, retarding cause.

February only saw fifteen miles added to the score on both sides. The going was terribly tough, but still it went on, the drills standing up to the strain magnificently with not even a scratch on their unthinkably hard surfaces.

Exmoor himself had ceased planning now and was on the actual scene of operations, at the rock face with Lacy by his side.

Between them they permitted no let-up. Both of them were here, there, and everywhere, checking movement towards the planned centre, supervising the removal of débris, deciding how and where to plunge the huge mechanical navvies so they could not possibly split the rock face at the wrong place. It was exacting, merciless work in the furious heat, stale air, and blinding light.

It went on, inexorably — and in a like manner Judith was putting forth the last scrap of her reserves into supervision of the last miles.

Exmoor's greatest fear was that neutronium might present itself again at this depth, due to the great pressure. If that happened he would have no Martin Astley to fall back upon, none of that scientific genius's calm appraisal of a problem. However, as yet, nothing of this nature presented itself — but there did come a time towards April, with 1,200 miles gained on each side, when the protesting drills seemed to reach their limit. To get any further was as impossible, it appeared, as trying to drive too long a screw through too tough a piece of wood. The drills did not chew; they just would not progress, even on the smallest diameter. And Canada, it appeared, was in the same boat. The Bore was finished except for 100 miles of barrier.

There was nothing for it but consultation — surely one of the most curious in history. A conference was held in the depths of both tunnels, at which Lovelace and all the important members of the Corporation were present, and their images and voices were transmitted by television through the barrier to the girl and men on the other side. They, likewise, had their own selves transmitted and so were present at the conference, even if it was by sort of proxy.

'You're our leading geologist in this side of the Bore, Mr. Fletcher,' Exmoor said, when he had opened the conference. 'What are we up against? What's stopping the last hundred miles from being broken down?'

Fletcher, a worthy successor to Henry Gaulter, shrugged.

'Pressure — purely and simply. You know how slow our progress became before we stopped. With every inch we go at this depth the pressure increases. It would be bad enough if we were boring into the earth alone — but as it is we have the appalling weight of the Atlantic Ocean above us as well.'

One or two men glanced upwards uneasily at the, as yet, unlined rocky roof. They jumped as Lovelace banged his fist on the portable table.

'All right, so we're fighting pressure. We've blasted our way through neutronium, the toughest thing known, and got away with it — even if there was trouble. Why can't we do the same again?'

'Because this isn't neutronium,' Fletcher answered seriously. 'It's simply an amalgam of the toughest rocks squeezed in from all sides and top and bottom. To get through it is like trying to drive a blunt pin through six inches of solid rubber.'

'Besides,' Judith put in, speaking from the televisor, 'one can't do as Mr. Astley did — drive electrons into the barrier to destroy it. It has them already. It's normal matter even though it's enormously tough.'

'Nuclear bombs?' Lovelace demanded. 'What's wrong with that?'

'Everything,' Exmoor sighed. 'Both sides have had trouble when they've fired nuclear charges, and we'd certainly get it if we released any at this depth. The incoming pressure is so vast that it would win the day in a moment if there were any stress, such as the shock produced by nuclear bombs. No, you can forget that — unless you want the ocean to come in on top of us.'

Lovelace shut his steel-trap mouth tightly shut and rubbed his bald head in vexation.

'There must be — something!' he

expostulated. 'Dammit, we can't be beaten now!'

'How about ordinary bombs, small charges?' suggested Judith, her eyes looking unnaturally big with worry and illness.

'No effect,' Exmoor grunted, and received a confirmatory nod from Jacobs, the leading acting physicist.

'Then we're stuck?' demanded one of the Canadian engineers, glaring impatiently from the screen.

'No — we're not stuck,' said Jacobs, the physicist, pensively. 'There's a way, I think, and we can thank Martin Astley for it. Even though he's dead he left plenty of notes, which I took over when I filled his position. It will interest all of you to know that he had worked out the principle of disintegration to a fine degree, mainly because he foresaw that the day would come when we'd run into something of vast pressure which even nuclear bombs wouldn't be able to take care of.'

Everybody was silent, their eyes on the physicist. He was a sallow-complexioned, brooding type of man with crisp black hair. He was aged about 45 and, as far as physics went, definitely knew his job. Exmoor was not sure whether he liked him or not, but not having had any close dealings with him he couldn't cast his vote definitely one way or the other.

'Well?' Exmoor asked at last, as Jacobs remained thoughtful. 'What idea did Astley have? Let's hear it.'

'I'll put it to you in non-technical language as far as possible. All of you know that matter is made up of atoms, electrons, protons, nucleus, and so forth. That's elementary knowledge. But not many of you may know that the electric charges — which is all these elements really are — can be cancelled out. Electrons are negative and protons positive. On the basis of opposite charges attract and like charges repel, matter is formed. But as long ago as 1934 there was discovered an opposite to the electron — the positron or positive electron . . . You're with me so far?'

'So far,' Exmoor agreed, glancing at the faces. 'Carry on, Jacobs.'

'The positrons, if produced in sufficient

quantities, are the sworn enemies of the protons — since both possess positive charges and repel each other. Destroy the protons in any matter and the whole set-up collapses, including the appearance of matter . . . Now to the point: Martin Astley, since the commencement of nuclear power as a definite thing, worked out how to produce streams of positrons all encompassed within a directional beam. By that I mean that as water is directed by a hosepipe, so in this case the beam directs and encloses the positron stream at one and the same time. Normally, before nuclear power made such advances, positrons could only be detected by natural occurrences — such as when cosmic rays fall on matter or when an atomic nucleus is bombarded by fast-moving particles. Astley is perfectly clear what he means in the draft designs he has drawn. The machines themselves — positron projectors as one might call them — very much resemble those with which he supplied electrons to that neutronium barrier.'

'You have the designs handy?' Judith

asked, and the physicist nodded.

'In my advance laboratory in the Bore here, Mrs. Exmoor.'

'And how long will it take to build a projector — or projectors — for the job we need?' Lovelace inquired.

'I should say about two weeks, since every engineering firm is geared up in readiness for any urgent demand we might make.'

'Then go ahead — fast as you can,' Lovelace ordered. 'That agreeable to you, Boyd?' He glanced across at Exmoor.

'Entirely — but first I'd like to see the designs for myself.'

'That can easily be done, Mr. Exmoor. Come to my advance laboratory the moment this conference is over.' Jacobs' eyes sharpened a little. 'There's nothing wrong with the designs; you can rely on me for that.'

Exmoor nodded. 'I do — most assuredly. I'm just wondering why Astley used borers for this tunnel job when he had disintegrators in mind. It would have immensely speeded up the job to simply disintegrate the rock instead of boring it

237

. . . Seems quite unlike Astley, somehow.'

'We don't know what was in his mind,' Jacobs said, shrugging. 'The fact remains we can make use of his invention now, when we really need it.'

'Which, to my mind, seems to take care of everything,' Lovelace said. 'I think we can close the meeting on that point — unless our Canadian friends have any observations to make?'

Apparently they had not — which officially brought the conference to a close. The rest, it seemed, was up to the genius of a man departed, and yet whose spirit still seemed to hover over the enterprise.

★ ★ ★

To Exmoor, who was not of course a trained scientist, the design of the positronic projectors seemed to be all that was required, a view shared by the other physicists on both sides of the Atlantic. So the order was given for four of the projectors to be rushed into manufacture immediately, and in the meantime each scientific team in the Bore selected, from their own members, men who would undergo rapid but thorough training in the handling of the projectors when completed.

Meantime, in the two weeks which were due to elapse until the projectors should be ready, there was a score of other jobs to be done — roof and wall plating, the first sleepers to be laid for the Cannon-Ball express, and small tasks by the hundred which kept both Exmoor and Judith extremely busy . . . The first two projectors were ready before they knew it — big, six-foot high things with businesslike snouts and air-sprung rubber wheels for traction. At a distance they looked remarkably like television cameras.

One was delivered to the British end and one to the Canadian. Jacobs, examining the British projector in company with Exmoor, pronounced himself entirely satisfied, and explained in detail many of the things that had Exmoor fogged completely.

'At the front,' the physicist explained, 'you see the snout from which the directional beam emanates. At the back here, in this massive lead container, is the uranium from which the nuclear energy, the positronic stream, is derived. As to how the positrons are actually created — it is simply a matter of vast heat, which causes the uranium to release the positrons. The radiation of the uranium itself, and the heat therefrom, are all masked by these lead and heat proof walls. To the operator there are only two things to remember — one is to switch on the power in the order of buttons shown on the control panel here, and the other is to direct the beam-nozzle towards the barrier to be disposed of.'

Exmoor looked at the rock face with its tracery of mineral veins; then he nodded.

'Fair enough, Jacobs. How soon do we start?'

'When the other two machines have been delivered. It will take two machines on each side to break the barrier; the area encompassed by one is hardly sufficient, and to move the machines about isn't too safe. Any unfortunate jar might cause a severe explosion. Naturally we want to prevent that possibility.'

'Naturally,' Exmoor conceded drily. 'All right, let me know when everything's ready, and I'll be here.'

He went on his way, spent the rest of the day doing various jobs, then in the evening contacted Judith. She looked even more wan than she had at the conference and Exmoor's heart sank when he saw her.

'Everything all right on your side, dear?' he asked, doing his best to sound brisk and cheerful.

'Proceeding to plan, general,' she smiled. 'The sooner we get these projectors ready and operating the better I'll like it. Our job will be finished then, as far as the Bore's concerned.'

'And then we take a holiday,' Exmoor said flatly. 'On that I am absolutely determined.'

'Yes . . . a holiday,' the girl agreed absently. 'Somewhere where there's blue sky, sunshine, and glorious fresh air. You've no idea how I've longed for it these past few weeks. More than I ever did before . . . Deep inside I know why.'

'I'll soon be with you, Judy, then it won't seem to be so hard a battle,' Exmoor said. 'Meantime, keep your chin up!'

'You know I'll do that . . . ' She gave a brave little smile and elevated her jaw slightly. Exmoor smiled back at her and put his thumbs up significantly. Then he cut the contact, and the smile died from his face as he did so. Judith was breaking up rapidly, and it was becoming increasingly impossible for him to keep a cheerful smile each time he saw her. He knew from this latest glimpse of her that when reaction did set in it would be shattering. It was even possible that Judith might collapse on the spot, conscious of the fact that, as far as the Bore was concerned, she had accomplished her mission.

Exmoor, in the full glory of health, rebelled against such a possibility. He wanted both Judy and himself to reap the reward of their endeavours, to spend the rest of their lives together and see the Bore as an established consequence of modern time. She must not die! That would be the bitterest blow of all. The Bore had taken everything so far: at least it must spare her. Exmoor prayed that night — a ritual in which he had only indulged perhaps three times in his life. He prayed that Judith might live . . . and go on living. Then when he fell asleep he dreamed about her, about the last barrier, and about Jacobs whom, for a reason he could not define, he did not wholly trust.

Then at length the second projectors were delivered — one to Britain and one to Canada. The men controlling them knew exactly what to do so it meant an end of all the delays; everything could go forward now to the finish. The finish! The central rendezvous when the two ends of the tunnel would at last join.

Officials of the Corporation assembled on the Canadian side; and on the British side Douglas Lovelace was heading a like party, together with representatives of the Government, the press, radio, and television. This was to be an epoch-making moment — the consummation of engineering genius.

'Ready?' asked Jacobs, looking at

Exmoor in the blaze of the searchlights.

'Go ahead,' Exmoor nodded, and at that Jacobs raised his hand in a signal. In the television screens the men on the Canadian side started up their projectors; on the British side the same thing happened. Four streams of positrons all hurled themselves against the adamant rock face, sweeping up and down and back and across, tracing a biting weave in the unthinkably hard substance, soundlessly and completely annihilating it wherever the beam touched. There was nothing but a faint buzzing note that gave no hint of the chaos being produced in molecular structure by the never-ending deluge of positrons.

The men watched with fascinated interest, as they did also on the Canadian side. It seemed impossible that the rock could be so easily destroyed and not leave a trace behind. There was something magic about it. The only thing that was left was a deep gouge where the ray had bitten, and the glowing edges where the normal rock remained — edges pinpointed with a myriad twinkling dots of purple light, rather like the glowing edge of a piece of paper that has not fully vanished in flame.

Deeper went the cuts, and deeper, carving out squares. When a complete square was made the rock did not fall out: it was simply 'positronized' out of existence.

'This is marvellous! Incredible!' declared Douglas Lovelace. 'No insufferable din; no thousands of tons of débris. Why on earth didn't Astley bring this invention to the front at the start?'

'A question which has puzzled me more than enough, D.L.,' Exmoor said, shrugging. 'Anyway, we've got it now so I suppose we ought to be satisfied.'

It was over an hour later when, from the Canadian side, there came an urgent alarm signal. The men on the British side, absorbed in the proceedings, looked up in surprise to behold the face of the Canadian physicist filling all the screen.

'Something's wrong, Mr. Jacobs!' he exclaimed. 'I had to cut off the projectors for a rest break, and it was then I saw something — in fact we all of us did.'

245

Jacobs raised a hand. The British projectors stopped also. In the screens mirroring the Canadian scene faces were anxious, including that of Judith.

'What seems to be the trouble?' Jacobs asked, surprised.

'It can soon be summed up,' Judith said; coming forward. 'The rock edges are still burning and disintegrating with the projectors switched off! How is it with you?'

Exmoor turned and looked at the rock face, then he started as he beheld those scintillating dots of purple light rippling around the edges of the sections already 'positronized'. As on the other side of the barrier, so here — with the projectors off!

'Well, what's the answer, Jacobs?' Exmoor demanded, turning to him. 'We can see these holes growing even as we watch — Look! Even in the holes themselves there are those dots of exploding light. I'm no scientist, but I know enough to assert that those light dots are molecular explosions, same as you can get in any laboratory test.'

'You're dead right there, Boyd,' Douglas Lovelace muttered, staring in fascination.

'It's the same with you, then?' Judith questioned anxiously.

'It is.' Exmoor glanced towards her screen; then he looked at Jacobs. 'I want an answer to this, Jacobs! We all do!'

The physicist was plainly caught on the hop. He just did not seem to know what to do with the situation. Exmoor looked at him in exasperation for a moment and then went over to the 'burning' rock to more closely examine it. He could hear a faint hissing sound, like hot ashes on which water has been sprinkled. Finally he touched the edge of the burning rock experimentally, intending to snuff out what seemed to be sparks. Instead his hand jolted back and a stinging pain crashed through his fingers. It reminded him of a time when, as a small boy, he had hit a hard cricket ball for six with a cheap bat.

He shook his hand fiercely and then stared at it in amazement. The first and second fingers had been amputated bloodlessly from the knuckle, leaving a rounded end covered with new, pink baby skin!

'I'll be damned!' he exclaimed in astonishment, and held the hand up for all to see. There was a stunned silence for a moment, both from the assembled men and those looking through the television screen.

'Bloodless surgery!' Jacobs exclaimed. 'The dream of the medical profession!'

'Never mind that,' Exmoor snapped. 'What's the cause of this and what are we going to do about it? The thing's got to be stopped somehow. Don't you realise that the rock is being eaten away on both sides of this barrier? Certainly it will complete the tunnel, but if it keeps on going it will also destroy it! The whole Bore will gradually be eaten away.'

'Yes,' Jacobs agreed. 'It certainly will — and there's nothing I can do about it.'

Exmoor stared at him, at the frozen grin on his face. Abruptly he realized what had been said — and with the realization he lunged forward and seized the physicist by the throat.

'Let's have it, Jacobs! You did this on

purpose, didn't you? Didn't you?'

'Correct,' the scientist agreed, pulling free of the iron grip. 'Martin Astley was not the inventor of this: it's the work of Rividin, the Austrian physicist, who died in curious circumstances a few years ago — '

'All right, cut it short,' Exmoor interrupted bitterly, glancing towards the Canadian screen and the startled faces thereon. 'So you're an enemy of the Bore, and the most dangerous one yet!'

Jacobs shrugged. 'I have no personal grudge, Exmoor — please understand that. I merely obey orders and use my scientific knowledge. I was ordered to find a way to use atomic chain reaction if ever a chance came. It did: the barrier gave me my opportunity. As the successor to Astley none of you suspected me.'

'What's the answer to this atomic chain reaction?' Lovelace demanded angrily. 'If you know what's good for you you'll tell us!'

'Even if I knew the answer I wouldn't give it, my friends, and so betray my own cause. There isn't an answer, unless

Rividin left one amongst his notes. I never concerned myself with looking. All I understand is the present effect of positron discharge, which has never been attempted before. It's interesting to notice that it will give bloodless surgery. That will be very interesting to the medical world.'

'Listen to me,' Exmoor commanded, his voice deliberate. 'You haven't told us everything, Jacobs! Suppose this atomic chain reaction goes on and on, as you mean it to do — There must come a time when it will reach Europe and the men behind your infernal Cause. Do you suppose they're going to allow it to continue, to eat away their buildings, their businesses, and the very ground under their feet? No; there must be somebody with an antidote to this business — and you're going to tell us who it is!'

'I think not!' Suddenly there was an automatic in Jacobs' hand. He had carefully arranged it so that he was on the outer edge of the circle of men. 'I'm going to leave you to sort out this little problem for yourself. I've done all I was ordered to do and now I'm going somewhere a bit safer. Don't any of you try to follow me if you know what's good for you!'

He began to back away, into the vast reaches of the tunnel. There were various men scattered about, certainly, but none of them took the chance of facing Jacobs' automatic. Exmoor hesitated, not quite sure what to do. He was aware of startled exclamations from the Canadian watchers, but he did not glance towards the screens.

One big fellow, tougher than the rest, moved forward suddenly as Jacobs came up the tunnel — and it was the last move he made. Jacobs' automatic spat and the man crashed on his face in the dirt . . . But in those few split seconds something else happened. One of the physicists in charge of No. 1 positron projector suddenly swung the huge instrument round on its unmounting and sighted it on Jacobs' backwardly retreating figure.

'Wait a minute!' Exmoor shouted hoarsely. 'Don't kill him! If you do we'll — '

Too late. The physicist pressed the button. There was no trace of a beam, but it was plain that the positronic power leapt the gap to where Jacobs was moving. He stopped suddenly in mid-stride, uttered a horrible scream, and then lurched sideways. Even as he did half of his body faded out of sight, then within seconds the rest of him went too in a puff of blue vapours. Around him the rocks started to glow with their pinpoints of purple light. Even the Steel-X plates, which had caught part of the radiation, were pitting and falling to crumbling pieces as the pinpoint twinkling expanded gradually.

'What the devil did you do that for?' Exmoor demanded of the physicist — and the young man looked in surprise from the machine.

'It seemed safer to have him out of the way, sir. Besides, he was dangerous.'

'And also vitally useful. He'd never have made it to freedom up the tunnel; somebody would have overpowered him. Then we could have made him tell us who knows the answer to this radiation, or whatever it is. Right now we're sunk!'

'Meaning what?' Lovelace snapped, striding forward and gripping Exmoor's arm. 'It's not like you to say a thing like that, Boyd! We'll master things somehow, same as we've mastered everything else. Dammit, we've only a hundred miles to go!'

Exmoor laughed shortly. 'Oh, our Bore will be finished, D.L. Have no fear of that! This chain reaction will make short work of the hundred miles of rock when it's biting like acid from each side — but at the same time it's going down and up. It's boring down into the volcanic regions of the earth, and eating its way up to the seabed! When the ocean and volcanic fire get together look out for fireworks!'

'Fanciful dreams, man! There are scientists amongst us — trained physicists! Just because Jacobs happened to pull a fast one with an invention devised by a scientist long dead, it does not mean nobody else on earth can do anything. What one man can do another can undo.'

'Whoever can undo this is probably in Europe,' Exmoor retorted. 'And we can never find him!'

'But . . .' Lovelace stopped, his hand scrubbing in frenzied vexation at his bald head.

'Can you suggest anything?' Exmoor demanded. 'Can any of us? Can any of you?' He looked at the screens mirroring the anxious faces of the Canadians.

'We might be able to think of something between us,' Judith said, not very hopefully. 'What about it, Boyd? Everything's set up ready for a conference. Let's have one.'

Exmoor reflected, then stared at the expanding area of atomic fire in the rock face. Finally he looked at his two neatly amputated fingers.

'All right,' he said quietly. 'It's that — or go bust, in more senses than one. Every man here, both Canadian and British — and by 'man' I mean you as well, Judith — had better start thinking harder than he's ever done in his life before. I don't want anybody who isn't a scientist. They'll only waste time. Agreed?'

Canada nodded. Douglas Lovelace looked at Exmoor seriously.

'This is where I retire, Boyd: I haven't a

scientific bone in my body.' He held out his hand. 'Good luck, boy — and by heaven you're going to need it.'

*　*　*

The conference, if one could call it that, began at 11:30 in the morning. At 11:30 that night it was still going on. Exmoor and Judith, not being expert scientists, could only offer helpful suggestions and then hear them torn to shreds by those men whose job it was to understand physics. They comprised about five men altogether — three Canadian and two British, and there was no doubt that they knew what they were talking about, and that they realized how completely they were up against it.

Exmoor watched and listened, forcing things back to calmness when tempers became heated. He gazed at the earnest, intellectual faces, shirt collars open and sleeves rolled up. He looked at the multitude of papers on which mathematics and algebraical symbols had been executed. He looked too, as did Judith on her side, at the vastly grown area of hole in the rock where, still glowing, it was hissing itself into extinction.

Strangely enough it was Harrison, the man who had volitalized Jacobs, who was emerging as the hero of the hour. Time and again he came up with a formula to which his brother scientists listened in profound appreciation. Time and again he cut other hypotheses to shreds — all the time coming nearer a feasible plan. Young and impulsive he undoubtedly was, but there was a profundity of reasoning in Jeffrey Harrison's twenty-nine year old brain. If a way was ever found out of this mess, Exmoor reflected, there was no doubt in his mind as to whom he would recommend as the next head physicist to the Bore Corporation.

'It seems to me,' Harrison said at last, active still in spite of twelve hours' gruelling work with hardly a break, 'that this disintegration business has opened up something new in physics. It would also seem that when an atom is blasted — as is happening here by chain process, one atom constantly firing off its neighbour — the atom does not completely disintegrate. That is shown by the fact that our instruments cannot detect any energy being given off, as there certainly would be were total disintegration present. What is happening is that there remains a shell of protons, the remains left from the onslaught of positrons. Matter as such has disappeared, but it is still there in shell-like form, too tenuous to be seen.'

'So what happens?' asked Judith wearily, lounging in a chair.

'This growing emptiness ahead of us is a region of positive universe stuff, as I'll call it, with no negative charges whatever. And as long as it remains as pure positive it will destroy everything in its track. The counterbalancing force of so much negative stuff around it is not sufficient to restore the normal positive-negative field. Something with a negative preponderance must react from the centre of the disturbance. Then, the negative influence will be radiated entirely from the centre, catch up with the disintegrating edges, and restore normalcy.'

Exmoor stirred from his chair as the

young scientist looked around on the work-weary group.

'Maybe you've doped something out at last, Harrison,' Exmoor said, 'but most of the technique is way above us . . . Can't you tell us what we do to put a — a negative influence in the centre of this disturbance?'

'Certainly I can.' Harrison was grinning now like a schoolboy who is about to perpetrate a trick. 'It's so simple that it hurts. All we need is something material — a rock, a stone, or even a lead pencil. We throw it into the area — magnetism and electrical processes will do the rest. It's not the size of the object that counts, but the electrical quota it possesses.'

'Oh,' Exmoor said, trying not to look or feel stupid.

'You don't understand, eh? Well, it's simple enough. Our piece of stone contains normal atomic charges, negative and positive? Right?'

'Check!' Exmoor agreed.

'Okay. Our stone is flung into the approximate centre of this growing hole in the rockery here — taking care not to touch the glowing edges. What happens? A scientific fact, even though it will look like a miracle. The piece of rock will set up an electrical field, which will gradually build up into an enormous positive potential. When positive and negative balance, in the space of maybe an hour, matter will abruptly return to normal because countless myriads of atoms will no longer be in the purely positive state. When they are back to normal the natural rock face will return and the trouble will be over.'

'In which case,' remarked the Canadian physicist, 'we shan't have gained anything. We'll be faced with unbreakable rock face once again.'

'I'm not so sure about that,' Harrison answered thoughtfully. 'It's possible that, after the hammering we've given the atomic basis of the rock, it will have been weakened considerably. Whether that is so or not, we've got to stop this spread of disintegration before it annihilates us, and even the very planet we live on. You agree, Mr. Exmoor?'

'Definitely,' Exmoor responded. 'And

allow me to congratulate you on a masterpiece of scientific reasoning.' He stirred himself into activity. 'When do we start?'

Harrison looked at the yawning maw of darkness edged with its pinpoints of purple light. The he replied quietly, 'I would say immediately. Every minute this trouble continues things get worse. I'll handle things from this end since I know exactly what's wanted. One of you,' — he glanced towards the television screen — 'will have to do your share from your own side.'

'I will,' Judith said promptly. 'What do I have to do?'

'Find a reasonable-sized piece of rock — ' Harrison looked about him and then dived suddenly forward. 'Here — like this.'

He held up a sizeable chunk of boulder in his hand. After a moment or two the girl was doing likewise. Out of the screen her eyes looked at Exmoor.

'One thing I must warn you of,' Harrison said. 'There may be an explosion when this business catches up with itself, but since it must be delayed by a few hours from its very nature — the time taken to build up an electrical field, I mean — we'll have plenty of time to get clear. So, the moment rock has been thrown, get away from the area quickly and watch developments. Understood?'

'Understood,' Judith said, and waited.

'Here it goes,' Harrison said, and threw the rock into the empty dark with its fringe of twinkling light. Nothing happened. There was a thud as the rock landed somewhere, presumably downwards, since the hole was already eating itself to an amazing depth.

'Do as I have done,' Harrison instructed — and Judith tossed her own rock into the blankness of the Canadian side.

That was all. Still nothing happened. Harrison, however, seemed satisfied.

'That's all we can do,' he said at length. 'Now let's get out and hope for the best . . . '

★　★　★

One hour and forty three minutes later, matter returned abruptly to the area of positronic disintegration. At that moment the atomic shells reached electrical balance with the negatively charged atoms of the two pieces of rock. Seismographs the world over recorded the immense shockwave. Rock slamming suddenly back to normal cracked and fissured, even crumbled in places, but did not give way. In mid-Atlantic the ocean boiled for a time, and then subsided. It marked the site where the last hundred miles of Atlantic bore remained as a barrier — but not for long. Along the galleries of the Canadian and British sides, Exmoor and Judith hurtled to the scene of the disturbance, carried by the shaft elevators and the electric railways, as fast as they could go.

They found rock face — on both sides, and measurements showed that one hundred miles of it still remained. Geiger counters, clicking like castanets, also showed that as yet the rock face was loaded with radioactivity, and as such a dangerous thing to tackle. The parties decontaminated themselves, and waited. A week, a fortnight — and then a month, before the radioactivity was pronounced by Harrison to be a negligible factor if insulated suits were worn.

Twin armies moved into action. With misgivings they tried the Astley drills, and the roar of delight that went up when the drills ploughed through the rock as easily as of yore could have been heard as far as the Poles. Just as Harrison had reasoned — though he admitted this fact was more or less guesswork on his behalf — the rock had been weakened by the positronic onslaught to which it had been subjected.

The drills went on! The teams of Steel-X men came behind them. The conveyors rattled away night and day. On and on, never pausing, Exmoor and Lacy exhorting their men to greater efforts; Judith doing the same on her own side. In a fortnight the barrier had decreased to fifty miles. May — June — July . . . Fifty miles — thirty miles — fifteen miles. August . . . Ten miles. Then came the never-to-be-forgotten afternoon of September 9, in the third year of the project, when the two teams could hear each others' drills through the last wafer of barrier.

And finally even that was gone. Grimy technicians stood and faced each other beside their huge drills. Two teams of men stretched away into the yawning gulfs. Two figures, tired but resolute, stood perched on opposite sides of a mountain of rubble — Exmoor and Judith . . .

The Land's End-Labrador Bore was finished . . . on this epoch-making day. Yet, even so, though the actual tunnelling had been accomplished, the original ten years allowed for the project were swallowed up in completing the final details.

The 2,500 mile long monorail track for the Cannonball Express was not completed until two years later, and it was another two before the first monorail trains ran upon it. In that time stations had been built, rest centres provided, galleries upon galleries of stores erected and opened, and pedestrian and traffic ways elevated far above the railway.

Officially, the Bore opened on the first day in February, ten years after the project had first commenced, with all the members of the Bore Corporation present — but looking and feeling a good deal older. Apart from the officials on the first monotrain trip to Labrador from Land's End, there was a sizeable slice of the normal community. Two of them, a boy and girl in their teens, sat in the rear observation car of the train as it left its destination and sped with ever-growing, bullet-like velocity through the colossal vista of gleaming, satiny Steel-X.

'Isn't it wonderful?' the girl said, over and over again, her young eyes bright with dreams. 'To think we're shooting under the Atlantic! Can you even start to picture the vision and imagination of the engineers who designed all this?'

'Yes — I can,' the young man replied, seriously, his eyes on the flashing lights as the train screamed onwards. 'I've read the history of the Bore — and a pretty amazing one it is. Makes me proud to be young in days like this. The leading light in it was a chap called Boyd Exmoor, as you probably know. He got a knighthood last year for the job he'd done.'

'*Mmmm*, I remember . . . Didn't he find something for the medical profession, too? Bloodless surgery, or something?'

'I believe so. Also a cure for radioactive cancer . . . His wife had radioactive cancer, you know, but according to the history of the Bore she got soaked in radiations from the last rock barrier — a barrier weakened by positrons. The radiations killed the disease and she recovered.'

'What are positrons?' the girl asked vaguely.

'I dunno. Doesn't matter, anyway . . . And say, are you going to stare into this tunnel the whole way to Labrador? How about a kiss for a change?'

The girl took her eyes from the bewildering, hurtling sides of the shaft and turned to look at the young man. He came within an ace of kissing her, then stopped as the door of the observation car suddenly clicked open. A tall, broad-shouldered man stood there, rugged faced and his grey eyes gave a understanding look.

'Er — we were just — ' the young man

started to say; but the big fellow interrupted him.

'Don't move, son. We can come back later. The last thing we'd do would be to spoil love's young dream.'

The woman with the grey eyes gave him a reproving look and then looked back towards the youngster whom she was holding by one hand.

'We'll look later on, dear,' she said. 'The car is occupied at the moment.'

She vanished from the doorway. The big fellow looked again at the two teenagers.

'Enjoy yourselves,' he smiled. 'And dream your dreams! That's what my wife and I did — that's what we'll wish our son to do as well. For such as you two youngsters the Bore was built . . . Bye-bye.'

The door closed again, but as it did so the two teenagers could not help but notice one thing — the right hand of the big fellow had two fingers amputated from the first knuckle.

CLIMATE INCORPORATED
THE FIVE MATCHBOXES
EXCEPT FOR ONE THING
BLACK MARIA, M.A.
ONE STEP TOO FAR
THE THIRTY-FIRST OF JUNE
THE FROZEN LIMIT
ONE REMAINED SEATED
THE MURDERED SCHOOLGIRL
SECRET OF THE RING
OTHER EYES WATCHING
I SPY . . .
FOOL'S PARADISE
DON'T TOUCH ME
THE FOURTH DOOR
THE SPIKED BOY
THE SLITHERERS
MAN OF TWO WORLDS

We do hope that you have enjoyed reading this large print book.

Did you know that all of our titles are available for purchase?

We publish a wide range of high quality large print books including:
Romances, Mysteries, Classics
General Fiction
Non Fiction and Westerns

Special interest titles available in large print are:
The Little Oxford Dictionary
Music Book, Song Book
Hymn Book, Service Book

Also available from us courtesy of Oxford University Press:
Young Readers' Dictionary
(large print edition)
Young Readers' Thesaurus
(large print edition)

For further information or a free brochure, please contact us at:
Ulverscroft Large Print Books Ltd.,
The Green, Bradgate Road, Anstey,
Leicester, LE7 7FU, England.
Tel: (00 44) **0116 236 4325**
Fax: (00 44) **0116 234 0205**

JOURNEY INTO TERROR

E. C. Tubb

The first exploratory expedition to Pluto returns with the Captain, Jules Carmodine, alone . . . What happened to the crew remains a mystery as Carmodine is suffering from amnesia, and mentally and physically broken in health. Later, although his health improves, the amnesia remains. Then, when Carmodine is forced to return to Pluto, he faces a journey into terror. He must remember what happened on that first mission — otherwise the second expedition will suffer exactly the same fate as the first . . .

SWARTHYFACE

Norman Lazenby

Kennedy Balfour, ex-RAF in post-war Britain, helps a frightened young woman on a train, but doesn't realise what he's getting into. He only knows that Delia Thomas is beautiful, and terrified of the man following her. Apparently the man, known as 'Swarthyface', is a criminal mastermind and his main target is the girl's father. And if Balfour persists in protecting the girl and her father, then one of them would die . . . and that someone might very well be himself . . .

THE SLITHERERS

John Russell Fearn

The obscure village of Coxwold had suddenly become the centre of attention of every daily newspaper. People from all over had descended upon it, investigating, questioning, and sending reports to London. Something had happened in a nearby wheat field which had reduced two normal, healthy men to insanity and death. The police, suspecting foul play, lacked any evidence. So what could it be that had driven the victims to madness? This was unlike any crime ever before recorded . . .

ESCAPE INTO SPACE

E. C. Tubb

Geldray, working for the government in building a starship, fears world destruction. So he privately plans to make the vessel a colonising project. Meanwhile, power-crazed Edward Smith intends to destroy all obstacles in his way — including Geldray, project Star and the politician Melgrath's reputation — in order to take over the government. Realising Smith's intentions, Geldray's last act is to launch the starship. Will the ship's crew succeed in escaping into space to find a new home amongst the stars?